MW01134429

Falling in Love with Chocolate

by _L. Elaine_

To DIVA
Deneen.
What a beautiful
surprise treat - You Are
A blessing to our lives -
Keep being on top of the
world sf thanks for
supporting me!

Acknowledgements

Hi Everyone! I finally made it to publication! As many have asked over the years, when will you publish your book? You know that book you typed/handwrote in 2008, set upon the chair and then filed on the shelf; the romance novel you wrote to see if you liked writing, and then proceeded to stare at for years? When you ask? Now! I dust off *Falling in Love with Chocolate* and am publishing it with the official launch on the day of love, this Valentine's Day - February 14, 2017.

I was scared what the world might do with my book, what might they demand of me next, and time flew by! A few months ago, I declared enough already! So, I got an amazing Coach (Author/Exec Coach Jen Coken) who fueled the smoke and flames until I got a full fire going!

This book is dedicated to my two grandmothers, Mary Juliette and Juanita, who passed away from this life after imparting to me much wisdom, including a love of reading that takes one to another world in any moment. I was truly blessed to be guided by their creativity and I pass it on.

Thank you for everything, and I mean everything, everyone provided that has gotten me to this point - the words of wisdom, assistance, suggestions, ideas, frowns/smiles, the yippeees, and oh nos! A special shout out to those who read excerpts, pushed me to the ledge, and were patient! To my fan club who always cheers for me—the writer (who secretly has been writing ten romance novels for almost ten years)! Please know that I am beyond thankful for you! Shout outs to: Denise M. for reading the first chapters of this book in the beginning, and then daily demanding I not stop until it was written (and that I let her read it day-by-day) ~ anything is possible! To Joan D., Barry Ch., and Rebecca for the publication advice; Coach Jen for leading the way in sharing your published book, processes and advice; my family, castaways and friends for listening to and supporting this endeavor; son Alex in sharing his talent and producing the book cover from my sketchy details; the crew of content and technical editors I didn't ask permission to say their names (Denise, Grace, Cricket); and for those I meant to mention by name and forgot in a senior moment!

In closing, I also acknowledge, YOU, the reader/conduit to creativity and imagination: whether we ever meet or not, thanks for reading this love story and creating an opportunity for people to fulfill on their dreams, share themselves with others and be self-expressed in this world!

Happy reading...

Introduction

....."Love is like swallowing hot chocolate before it has cooled off. It takes you by surprise at first, but keeps you warm for a long time." – Anonymous

Falling in Love with Chocolate is the light-hearted story of two people from different worlds, Juan Carlos and Lacey, who find one another on vacation in a romantic medieval city...They had totally different motivations and agendas for life, yet they fall in love; and in an unexpected twist of fate that surrounds eating chocolates, they learn to believe in the importance of falling in love and staying there before it is too late.

I created this first book about a place that is near and dear to my heart: Bruges, Belgium. When I first traveled to this medieval city decades ago, I thought it was the most romantic place I'd been. So of course, my first book of love had to take place in Bruges: the perfect place to fall in love!

To give you a little background into the Gutiérrez family and dynasty. I got the idea while weaving my way through Spain on holiday in 2007. I learned Spain is at times the largest producer of olive oil in the world (in competition with Italy); and so, I thought what a fun idea to create a wealthy family and place it in the countryside of Southern Spain, near the capital city of the Jaen, Andalusia! Jaen is said to be the least known of the eight provincial capitals, with its beautiful mountains as a backdrop, and surrounding miles and miles of olive tree groves. More on Jaen and the region will be shared in the upcoming love stories of the Gutiérrez brothers.

Read on and begin to delve into La Familia Gutiérrez in book one of the *Dynasty of Love* series: *Falling in Love with Chocolate*.

Chapter 1

"Life is like a box of chocolates - you never know what you're going to get."
~ *Forrest Gump in "Forrest Gump" (1994)*

As Lacey Blake quietly walked back to the car wiping away her grieving tears, she remembered many of the life lessons that her grandmother Maria had imparted over her thirty-two years of life. Maria, as she preferred Lacey call her once she turned eighteen, was her last living relative, and light of Lacey's life. Her last days were spent in quiet serenity within her home, her devoted granddaughter by her side. She had a calming grace and unconditional love for family. She lived to be one hundred four years old and never stopped being a woman on the go. She was an inspiration in so many ways.

In years past Maria and Lacey came to this very spot on the annual pilgrimage to lay flowers on the graves of loved ones in memorial. Maria always loved this place as it reminded her of the peace God promised. Now here her body would remain, but her spirit was in heaven eating chocolates galore. As Lacey said goodbye, all she felt was a need to escape and never return. She knew she owed more to her grandmother, whom devoted so much to raising another lost angel, but she just did not want to feel anything anymore.

Maria watched over her son's only child from a young age, chose to expose her to the world of travel and cultivated a love of all things chocolate. She often had a "pearl of wisdom" to share and it usually ended in a saying about chocolate. A favorite was a spin on a quote from an infamous cartoon: all I really need is love, but a little chocolate never hurts. Lacey was convinced that love hurt too much, so why bother. Everyone was born and at some inopportune moment they died...leaving behind at least one broken heart. Her heart had been broken too many times.

For the last six months while Maria ailed, the house became a sanctuary where the two women peacefully co-existed. Lacey gladly quit her job as an executive assistant to tend to her grandmother's every need. She prepared all the meals and brought them to Maria on the sunroom porch while nature looked on. Many an hour was spent with her reading to Maria in multiple languages. Always there were a few pieces of chocolate at hand.

Lacey refused to travel while Maria was homebound, so instead they poured through magazines displaying decadent delights to order.

A couple of days later a shipment would arrive, tea would be prepared, a good book selected, and time would pass until the box was empty. The last box of chocolates arrived just three days ago. Lacey thought all her tears were shed until the doorbell rang and she noticed the package sitting on the doorstep. She could not remember ordering anything but so much had been going on over the last few weeks. As she tore into the box, she saw the label for European truffles. Tears welled up and she felt her heart being pierced with a knife. As she closed the door the first tear slid down her cheek. She walked with the box to the sunroom, set it on the tray and cried again for the times lost.

As if going through the motions, she went into the kitchen and prepared a cup of herbal tea. With tea in hand she pulled a familiar book off the shelf and sat down in front of the box of truffles. She picked out the selections Maria had requested careful not to cry into the box. It was her grandmother's dying wish that they order chocolates to celebrate the arrival of Fall. Maria's sense of adventure always made her select a few flavors they had never previously ordered. There was always a reason to have chocolate. Lacey again felt a pang of hurt as she bit into a lemon meringue truffle. It was made of white chocolate and tart lemon. She really did not taste it as she stared out into the flower garden.

After a while, Lacey tried to think about how long she sat in the lounger. Some hours must have gone by because the sun was setting. Looking down into the box she realized there was just one truffle left to taste. It was a pumpkin spice truffle. She recalled her exact conversation with Maria. In honor of the new fall season fast approaching, Maria felt they just had to try the pumpkin flavor ~ it seemed natural to celebrate harvest, which on any farm included pumpkins.

Gazing out the window into the backyard, Lacey noticed the leaves had yet to begin their descent to the ground, but the process was underway. Their time to die was coming too. Maria often repeated to Lacey "to everything there is a season." Straight out of Ecclesiastes Chapter 3 she could recite from memory the verse that was said at the funeral. Her grandmother knew her season was coming to an end.

It would be a long time before she again sat here in this place. It was time to uproot and leave. She had broken down, wept, had a last laugh and mourned. Now she had to build up her wall of resistance. For one to implement an iron clad refusal to accept love and its resultant hurt was the first step to healing. Lacey felt she had lost everyone in her short lifetime. But she still had chocolate as a consolation. One could learn a lot by eating chocolate…chocolate is love, and there is always plenty of chocolate in the world to keep one craving more, more, more…as each blissful taste melts in your mouth. Lacey's favorite quote was one from an unknown author…and her grandmother never liked it: *forget love, I'd rather fall in chocolate.*

******

Lacey stepped off the plane into the airport of Belgium's capital city, Brussels. The transatlantic flight was uneventful as everyone tried to sleep into the morning. The six-hour time difference was painful to her since it was still the middle of the night back home. Even though anxious to leave the city behind and get on to her desired destination, she was distracted by all the choices of Belgium chocolate at airport stands. There were too many choices and there would be plenty of time to acquire chocolate later, so she decided to head to baggage claim and retrieve her lone piece of luggage.

October could be a chilly month in this part of Europe. Lacey was hopeful when she left home that it would still be warm. If not, she was prepared to buy a few items to tide her over while she enjoyed her month of chocolate restoration. Money was no object since her trust fund was bestowed on her when she turned twenty-five. With Maria's death, even more wealth was amassed, including the farm estate that boosted her portfolio further into the millions. None of that mattered to her. What mattered was leaving the painful memories behind. She was not yet sure what to do with Maria's assets, but she knew she could never sell the house where she grew up.

The choice of where to go to get her life back together and find purpose was not a hard one. Europe had the best chocolates. There were all different types from the sinfully rich dark to the purest vanilla-hued white. But Belgium chocolates were her favorite. She could have easily stayed in Brussels and sampled its delights one corner at a time. City life was too busy for this trip, and she needed quiet time to meander and explore, relax and release. The plan is to spend a month in Bruges. The smaller and quaint Medieval city was the perfect escape-known as the Venice of the North. There were chocolate shops, canals, museums, culture and solitude just around each corner. It always held a special place in Maria's heart, and in Lacey's.

Lacey was a blessing to the whole family as a mid-life surprise baby to parents who never expected to have a child, let alone a precious little girl to spoil...Maria, an only child herself, was seventy-two years old when she was born. Lacey never met her grandfather, Harvey, who died before she arrived on the scene. She was named after Maria's obsession with tatting, a form of making lace. That was a secondary reason to come for solace to Bruges—famous for its lace makers. From the time she was two, Lacey was full of adventure and loved to sit in Maria's dining room and savor the surprise chocolates shared from around the world.

At the age of eight, both Lacey's parents died in a terrible car accident. Despite the age differences, the family was close knit until the tragic night of the storm. There were no siblings to raise a young child, so Maria took Lacey into her home and raised her by sharing wonderful memories of Harvey, her parents, world travels, and life experiences. No matter how much Maria loved and treasured her, she always felt abandoned by her parents because they died without her. She felt an overwhelming sense of guilt because they might have never died if she had just gone home that night.

The night of the accident Lacey had begged her grandmother to let her stay over at her house— she never wanted to go home when she could stay with Maria. Her parents were coming to get her on the way home from a play. When they arrived to pick her up, she pretended to be asleep so she could stay. She could still hear her father's voice. He was tired so he opted not to try to wake her or pick her up and put her into the car. They planned to come back in the morning. On the way home, rain was pouring down in sheets. Per the police reports, as her parents' car turned onto on a winding road it skidded out of control and into an embankment. Neither of them survived the crash. Four days later, Lacey attended their funeral with tears in her eyes. Her parents were buried in the cemetery in a plot next to Grandpa Harvey. Lacey tried to climb into the grave as she screamed and yelled that they should take her with them now...After all these years, the memory still felt so real.

Just a few more minutes and Lacey would get her train. It was so awesome that trains left the airport terminal every 30 minutes. European rail was so advanced in comparison to those in the United States. In about two hours she would be in Bruges. A couple more hours after that and she would be all checked in and traipsing down to the main square in search of her favorite chocolate morsels, including the Bruges Swan.

******

Juan Carlos snapped the cell phone shut in anger. Imposed vacation - how could the Board of Directors do this to him? They had systematically locked him out of his own multi-national corporation for the next six weeks. Greg Martin, his chief advisor and long-time friend, had noted it was an imposed vacation so that he would stop snapping at the staff and expecting them to live and die work. They thought "if he could just understand the joys people felt on vacation then he would understand their need to spend time with family, and maybe he would not be so demanding." Greg even suggested Juan Carlos have a brief love affair to distract himself. Nothing serious, yet it would keep him occupied and not thinking about what was going on back in the office. Who wanted to escape work? Juan Carlos never understood why people did not enjoy working. He surely felt his blood boiling with no plan on how to spend his days and nights.

He had to know what was going on with the negotiations for his latest acquisition. Just a few more hours of access to his plush office that occupied prime real estate in Barcelona's business district would help him shut down and relax. In his own element, with noise and distraction, he was driven to succeed. It was the only joy in his life right now.

That morning at dawn, Greg sent a courier with plane tickets and instructions. Juan Carlos was headed to Belgium on business. He boarded the plane never questioning Greg's rationale. When he arrived at Brussels Airport a driver was awaiting him. He suspected that there was an impending business meeting. He was whisked off to the small town of Bruges where he now stood. He had never been here before. Most often when in Belgium it was for a quick business trip in Brussels, an international city of diversity. He called Greg when after checking into the hotel he realized there were no messages outlining his next steps. He assumed his business meeting would take place in the early afternoon. Greg seemed uncomfortable delivering the Board's message. Since he trusted Greg he asked his advice. Greg hesitated but then acknowledged that it was time for his boss to rejuvenate.

Frustration plagued the lines of Juan Carlos' face. He had to come up with a plan to convince the Board to change their mind. He thought to himself, maybe I will just spend the weekend here. The Board would then see they could not function efficiently without him being in the office and call him home. They would offer apologies and try to mollify him with excuses as to why they erred. He might even stay a few extra days to make them panic. When he arrived back in Spain and retook the helm they would recant their harsh assessment of his persona. He crossed the square and sat down in an outdoor café. Barcelona, situated along the Mediterranean coast, seemed worlds away from this Medieval town. It was like walking back in time. Since crossing over the small bridge into town, he noticed people everywhere riding bicycles. He thought to himself how long had it been since he had been on a bicycle. It had been so long he could not remember. Coming to his mind more immediately was his sporty, little, black BMW. It is sleek and fast as it darts in and out of traffic on the busy cosmopolitan streets back home. Propelling oneself without the purr of a motor left a lot to be desired.

Chapter 2

"My favorite thing in the world is a box of fine European chocolates which is, for sure, better than sex." ~*Alicia Silverstone*

Juan Carlos was still sitting in the café finishing up a strong cup of espresso when he gazed across the square. Instinct made him zone in on a woman who stopped in front of a chocolate shop. It took one brief moment to see her—all of her. She had brown hair with ringlets of curls that spiraled around her angelic, heart-shaped face. She had taken off her hat briefly to gaze into the window before putting it back on. She had her hair tied up and he hoped once freed it would cascade down her back. She had a body with curves that made him stir. As she turned to look around the square her eyes caught the sunlight and he stopped breathing. They twinkled amber in color and oozed liquid gold. It was like staring into the eyes of a cat. They sizzled with fire and he felt obsession start to build. She was looking for something, and he had just found his next distraction. This woman looked out of place. She was foreign, maybe American. Watching indecision as it played across her face intrigued him. Lust shot through him with a force he had never felt before. He needed to meet her; he had to have her in his bed. An idea surfaced in his brain. It was most likely being driven by a much lower part of his body, but at least it was a better alternative to his former angry thoughts.

Maybe Greg was right. A weekend tryst might quell his need to work. So much for contemplating global acquisitions while he explores Bruges on his own. The woman turned back around and considered the shop window. She then walked into the store. Work was the furthest thing from his mind. After all Bruges, should be discovered in the company of others!

With a sense of purpose he had not felt in weeks, Juan Carlos dropped money and a tip to cover his service on the table and crossed the square. He stopped just in front of the window. He saw the object of his latest desire having a conversation with the storekeeper as she gazed intently at the truffles in the glass cases. His gaze drifted to peruse her left hand where he noticed no wedding ring. Juan Carlos stepped inside wondering if he could convince her to look at him the way she did chocolate.

As Lacey made choices about her first of many chocolate purchases, she heard the store door chimes announce the next entrant into the chocolate haven. She was totally not interested in who might have come along to compete for her chocolate selections. She had chosen this store with great care after looking around the square a few minutes before and seeing nothing else of more compelling interest. This shop had a phenomenal window display. Within its walls were even more enticing varieties. She had strolled only a little way from her hotel and discovered true bliss!

Half listening Lacey heard a gentleman say, "¡Buenas tardes Senor y Senorita! ?Usted habla español?" She then thought to herself surely, he had not included her in his salutation. But there was no one else other than the three of them in the shop front. He was definitely speaking Spanish in native tongue. The shopkeeper switched from Flemish to English and said, "No sir. I only speak very little Spanish, but I am fluid in French, English and my native Flemish (Dutch)." Then the man said, "Usted es la cosa más bella que he visto." Lacey immediately raised her head to assess this man. He was a very handsome Spaniard of dark olive skin tone, wavy black hair just barely tamed at his neckline, and icy blue eyes pinning her to where she stood. Did she hear right? Did he really say that she was the most beautiful thing he had ever seen? Was he joking? Her quick appraisal as they looked intently at each other said he was far from playing a game. He obviously knew understood what he said and she could see desire in his eyes.

She smiled and her gaze swept down his body as she appreciated his strong shoulders and solid build. Then she looked away returning her interest to the chocolates below her fingers. She tried to steady her breathing and slow her heart rate. The shop keeper asked the man if he spoke English and how he might be of help. The stranger switched to English and replied in a deep masculine voice, "yes, I am looking to purchase a box of chocolates as a gift to an acquaintance. Lacey felt a slight pang of agitation as she somehow wished a man had been that thoughtful to think of her. "Oh well," she sighed "maybe someday. Right now she did not want any strings, relationships or acquaintances.

Quiet ensued in the confines of those four walls of concrete and glass. Lacey refocused her attention on filling her box of favorites. Awareness kicked in when she felt the presence of the stranger near her. Without averting her eyes to check, she would swear the stranger was staring at her. He cleared his throat and Lacey jumped. He was right next to her when he said "you look like an everyday expert on chocolate."

Lacey turned and looked into the face of a man who smiled at her as if she were a piece of meat he was about to devour. His eyes had turned a darker shade of blue. He was brooding.

Lacey said "well I do know a little bit about chocolate. It is my favorite treat in life."

With a heart-stopping smile he said "might you tell me which ones are your favorites and I will also buy them for my gift. I need a woman's touch so I make the perfect choices and do not disappoint." Yeah right, who could ever be disappointed with him. Refraining from making that public comment, Lacey looked at him trying to decipher if he was serious or not in seeking her assistance. Men had all kinds of agendas and she was wary of his motivation and sexy smile. She paused a moment longer as he looked almost to be pleading with for her help. A man this gorgeous did not beg. Lacey looked across the room at the shop keeper. He was busying himself adjusting displays and was no longer engaged in providing active assistance.

With a deep sigh of resignation, Lacey said in a mix of Spanish and English "alright, si senor, I will help you." Then she asked what language he would prefer she communicate. Juan Carlos said English was fine. Lacey quickly switched to all English and went about explaining her choices and why they mattered to her.

Juan Carlos thought to himself he was quite intrigued with this woman and for the first time in many months he felt as if he was in no rush to go anywhere or do anything else. When it appeared both their boxes were full, they headed toward the register to pay for the goodies. The store keeper magically reappeared. Juan Carlos asked that his box be wrapped as a gift. Lacey was again reminded that it was not about her. This man obviously had someone special in his life. With a complete package like him, he could have any woman he chose and even a different one every day of the week. As he made his purchases, Lacey busied herself reading the ingredients listings on the prepackaged chocolates. If given the choice, she rarely bought any kind of prepackaged chocolates. When he was finished, he approached her. She felt compelled to make eye contact with him. Gosh his eyes mesmerized her and she lost track of rational thought. Thank goodness this was goodbye because she did not need to give anyone that kind of power over her.

He reached out a hand to her and said "I've been so rude. Please forgive me." Lacey was puzzled and said "how so, senor?"

"When I finished making my purchase, I realized I wanted to say thank you. But then I thought here this woman has taken great pains to help me, and I have not formally introduced myself. My name is Juan Carlos Gutiérrez."

Lacey placed her hand gently into his and said "it is very nice to meet you." Feeling her heartbeat pick up to an erratic pace, she let go.

"Thank you for spending time to assist me."

Lacey then turned back to pick up her box of chocolates and move toward the register. Juan Carlos stepped into her path. "Senora, you did not give me your name."

Lacey quickly reassessed the exchange, smiled and said "Senor now it is I who has been impolite to you. I apologize. My name is Lacey Blake."

With no mistake, he was totally focused on her. "It is a pleasure to meet you, Lacey Blake. Please let me express my gratitude to you by sharing with me a cup of hot chocolate at the café just across the square."

"No senor, it is not necessary."

He gave her another heart stopping smile. "It would make me feel better. After all I owe you and I do not like to feel I'm indebted to anyone."

She took note of how adamant he was as he spoke that statement. She was sure there was a story linked to it. Already in chocolate withdrawal and needing strength, she popped a chocolate into her mouth and savored how it melted on her tongue. With the lightest touch, she licked her lips. Oh, how she loved chocolate.

The shop keeper cleared his throat and she remembered the chocolate she so desperately needed to purchase, including the one she had just consumed. Two men stared at her expecting an immediate decision.

She gazed at Juan Carlos. "Yes, I will allow you to buy me hot chocolate. But first, I need to pay for my purchases. She noticed his lips curving upward as she moved to the counter. After paying, the shop keeper smiled, wished them both a nice day, and noted they should come again often to take advantage of the specials. Obviously, he appreciated the exchange between Juan Carlos and her as if romance was in bloom.

Lacey gave him a quick smile, her thanks, and turned around feeling trapped like a bug in a spider's web. *My, my, my what a tangled web!* Would having hot chocolate with this man be enough to quell her nerves? Oh, those eyes were making her forget everything else. As Juan

Carlos held the door for her, she felt like she was in a trance and all rational thought had eluded her mind, body and soul. He would lead and she would follow. *Let's just hope all he wants is to repay her gratitude with a hot cocoa.*

He purposefully asked for a table indoors so he could focus on Lacey. The hostess showed them to a table in the corner of the café. Juan Carlos noticed the intimate setting of the interior. They were relatively alone as most often Europeans chose to sit outside this time of the year. Until winter set in people were out soaking up the remaining warmth of the sun. Inside it was the perfect backdrop to seduce this woman. She seemed hesitant but she still had that sparkle in her eyes. He saw adventure there as she anticipated his next move.

"So, do you still want hot chocolate or something else."

"Oh yes, I very much want hot chocolate." She lightly laughed. He signaled the server over and ordered two hot chocolates.

Moments later the server brought their hot chocolates. Impatient to sip the creamy, rich liquid, she peered down into the frothy chocolate and licked her lips. He noticed she had this way of sticking her tongue out that was driving him mad. Mesmerized over the way she sipped he wondered to himself how anyone could look so sexy drinking from a cup. He envied the mug beneath her slender fingers being raised again to her lush pink lips.

"So, what brings you to Bruges, senor?"

"Please Lacey, call me Juan Carlos."

She blushed. "Yes of course. Juan Carlos, what brings you to Bruges?"

He took a quick gulp of hot liquid. "Let's just say I'm here for a long, leisurely weekend."

She examined his eyes and saw a moment of emotion. Almost immediately whatever Lacey thought she noticed there disappeared and he gave her a heart stopping smile.

"This is my first time here. I want to explore this quaint little town."

"It is a wonderful place."

"Lacey, do you live here in Bruges?"

"Oh, no, I am just an avid tourist."

"Really? Have you ever been here before?"

"Yes, numerous times. It is one of my favorite places to visit."

"If you do not mind my asking. Why is it so special to you?"

By the time Lacey finished explaining her passion for Bruges her hot chocolate was finished. Not ready to let her go, he had to do something. He did not want to intimidate her. And he got the impression she was leery of people. "Would you like another cup of chocolate?"

"No thank you. I really must be going. Thank you for this." She waved her hand over the cup. He reached out and touched her hand. She felt hotter than the chocolate he had just consumed. That simple touch had seared his chest. What is it about this woman that had him so unsure of himself?

In a smooth and thick accent he spoke. "Lacey, you cannot imagine how much fun it has been spending this last hour in your company."

Lacey just stared back at him. She was feeling too much with him this close. All she wanted to do was escape. Or did she? Cutting into her thoughts she heard him break the silence.

"Not to be too forward…Over the next few days, I want you to show me Bruges. To see it through your eyes would be a rare indulgence—one I very much want to experience."

"Senor, I am flattered but I am no tour guide. I am not qualified to be your guide."

With lips and a body that was guiding him toward sin, he doubted she knew how good she could be. "Have dinner with me? You can think it over and give me your response. I am not used to being alone. To be honest, it has been a long time since I have had any free time. I am usually consumed with work."

Lacey never felt much at a loss of words. But she was full of indecision right now. Again, he broke her thoughts.

"To wonder off on my own will drive me insane. I will end up resenting this town and I would like to avoid that if possible. You seem to have sparked my imagination, which is rare. On the surface, Bruges looks to me like it should not exist anymore. Yet, I see a sense of contentment in the faces of the people. They exhibit a happy nature. Surely they are not all tourists like me."

How sad his life sounded. Lacey felt a definite need to inquire more. "Juan Carlos, what kind of work do you do? It sounds like you do not know how to enjoy life."

He blanked his face and showed no emotion. "You are right. I work in business. That's all the more reason for you to take me on for a few days as a project. You are here through the weekend, no?" He felt compelled to do whatever it took to see her again. One moment at a time, one step at a time. He was sure they would have a memorable time.

Lacey could not tell whether he told truth or lies. Did it matter? She was unsure of herself and what to do. He looked patient in awaiting a response. "Yes, I am here for a while. Will you give me a moment to think?"

"But of course."

As hard as it was, she turned her attention away from him. Should she go to dinner? She wanted to, but she did not want to be a tour guide. After such a sad pronouncement, Lacey felt sorry for him. Then again, she did not think such a handsome and powerful man would appreciate her assessment. There was so much more to life than work. His personality was very hard to resist. He seemed to be controlling his pleasure.

She wondered what he would be like unrestrained and carefree. Would he see the passion and romance Bruges held? Even though she had never shared this place with a man, most of her hesitation in accepting his offers was to protect herself from falling in love and being left behind to pick up the pieces. Being hurt would destroy her admiration of this place. Oh, but what could it hurt to have dinner. That was a great way to forestall having to decide. It would buy her time to figure out how to say no to being his tour guide.

"Okay Juan Carlos, I will have dinner with you. However, I do not yet have a final decision on your request that I be your guide."

"I am content with allowing you more time. We can discuss it at dinner. Since I am new in town, where might you suggest we dine this evening?"

As they discussed the many options, they discovered they were both staying at the same luxury accommodations, *The Landhuis Resort*, and agreed to meet for dinner in the lobby. The hotel name translated from Dutch to English to mean the country house. Lacey was not overly comfortable with the fact that coincidentally they were staying in the same place. It appeared to be another stroke of fate that had thrown them together. Did she trust herself to not fall into his tempting arms? She was hot and bothered thinking about what it would be like to sample him, put her hands on his strong chest, taste the remnant of hot chocolate on his lips. Oh, she had to get a grip on these fantasies. He offered to escort her back to the Landhuis. She made a pretense of having more errands and off she went.

When they parted, Juan Carlos realized it was the perfect time for a siesta. Oh, how he wished she were going to siesta with him. Grinning to himself he could just imagine there would not be much sleeping to occupy the afternoon hours if she were by his side. Soon enough.

On her way back to the Landhuis, Lacey contemplated what she should do until dinner. She was way off schedule because of her flight. Also, she did not get in her five-mile run today and she was starting to crash. She needed a nap to refresh…ah, a siesta was in order!

When she returned to her room, she was restless. Every time she stood still for a few minutes, she could feel her heart beating and her mind straying back to him. *This has to stop. It's just dinner.* She needed exercise. So, she changed into her racer swimsuit and cover up and headed off for the indoor lap pool. About thirty laps and she would be restored.

There was no one else at the pool. She stripped off her gauzy cover up and flip flops. As she did so she thought about Juan Carlos assisting her with each layer. *Whoa, she needed to regain some control.* She dropped her stuff on the nearest lounger and plunged into the pool. Lap one: what does he want…Lap two: of all the places, how is it he is staying at the same hotel…Lap ten: what would his lips feel like against hers…Lap fifteen: *this is no use, I cannot forget him.* Lacey got out of the pool, collected her stuff, and went back to her room.

As soon as she entered the suite she noticed a gift bag on the coffee table. There was a note attached. She moved tentatively toward the gift. Only one person could have sent this package to her. Juan Carlos. With shaky hands, she unfolded the note… "looking forward to dinner. See you at nine." Inside the bag was the exact same box of chocolates she helped him pick out as a gift. Not able to resist the call of untouched chocolates, she opened the box and chose a dark chocolate hazel nut. It was very thoughtful of him to give her this gift. Did he understand that chocolates hold an important place in her life. She smiled and headed for the shower as the chocolate melted off her tongue. Yummy. *Arousal, seduction, gifts…this is so not a part of my relaxation plan.*

Lacey emerged from the steamy bathroom. A hot shower always brings prospective. She was safely tucked into one of the luxury robes provided for each hotel guest. She laid out her little black dress and strappy, black sandals. With plenty of time to calm her anticipation before getting dressed for dinner, she took a strawberry cream truffle and slid beneath the covers. Before she knew it, she fell into a deep sleep.

Lacey heard an insistent knock at the door. She felt like she was fighting to come out of a hazy fog. Then she realized she was asleep. Her eyes opened and she looked around to an unfamiliar setting. The knocking continued. She sat up. She was still in bed and exhausted. She stumbled into her slippers and went to the door. Through the peep hole she saw a handsome face, and then it hit her it was Juan Carlos. She thought she dreamed their meeting. She spun around remembering her nakedness beneath the robe. Her gaze caught sight of the glow of the clock as it said quarter past nine.

Oh no...I've overslept and missed meeting him in the lobby at nine. Running a hand through her hair and hoping he would not get the wrong idea by her current choice of dress (or undress), she spun around and opened the suite door.

When Lacey had not shown up in the lobby as planned, he refused to worry that she was in distress or they had mixed their signals where to meet. He remembered all the details of the day since they had met and had been replaying them over and over in his mind. He was sure this was the right room as a result of the favors he called in to get her room number so the chocolates could be delivered hours ago. "Hmmm, maybe she has changed her mind." Juan Carlos was just getting ready to knock on the door again when it opened.

He was not usually one to gawk, but wow. From her hips, he forced his eyes to sweep upward. He wondered if this was an invitation to come in. By the time his gaze settled on her face, he saw the definite color in her cheeks. She was clearly embarrassed, but also aglow in the shadows. His first thought at her not being in the lobby was that she's stood him up. Now he recognized she must have just awoken.

With his fingers, Juan Carlos wanted to follow the line where the terry cloth robe denied his vision to see; exploration of what lay beneath. Was she naked? Did she have on some silky, slinky garment? Returning his focus back to her lips, he heard her say "Juan Carlos, please forgive me for not meeting you."

"You did not change your mind about dinner, no?"

"No. With the jet lag and a hot shower, I fell asleep. Give me ten minutes and I will be ready."

"Do you want me to wait here? You know you could invite me in and we could order room service." He smiled and she gave him a panicked look.

"I do not think it would be appropriate for me to entertain you in my room. Just give me ten minutes. I'll see you in the lobby." Lacey slammed the door in his face.

How abrupt that she shut him out. She'd just displayed a little more of her personality. He was not sure why he found it encouraging that she did not just give in to him. But he afforded her more respect for how she'd 'handled' him. Turning on his heel he decided to do as she asked and wait for her in the lobby. There would be plenty of time for seduction. He did not lose any conquest and he did not take advantage of women. She would come willingly into his arms.

She appeared in the lobby right on time. She was dressed in a simple, yet elegant black dress. It was sleeveless with a scooped neck. Her hair was pulled into a clip with her curls trying to escape. At her neck was a single teardrop necklace that held a piece of amber suspended in the center. Just the frisson in the air between them made him want to run to her and take her in his arms to brand her with his kiss. He had to restrain the urge to show everyone she was his woman. Such possessiveness was not like him. They'd just met. Coming to grips with the idea that it was too soon, he did not move.

As she approached he heard the click, click of her strappy heeled sandals. "You are beautiful," he said as he bent his head to kiss both her cheeks.

"Thank you. I have to tell you though that I am worn out after my travels."

"Mi querida, if this is how beautiful you look when you are tired, I fear you will stop traffic when you are at your best."

Lacey did not like being the center of attention on an ordinary day. Today, with this man who possessed looks to cause his own traffic jam, she was even less at ease. She thought it the best course to change the subject. "So, senor, where are we having dinner."

"Well I thought we should dine here at the hotel's restaurant. It is supposed to have a renowned chef, great menu, and select wine list."

"Sounds perfect! I did not know how to dress, but I figured I could not go wrong in simple black."

"You could wear anything or nothing and still look fabulous."

She could not hide the blush that sent flames to her face and other parts of her anatomy. "You unnerve me with your compliments, senor."

"Please, let us make a deal Lacey? If you stop calling me senor, then I will refrain from commenting on how scrumptious you appear to me."

"It's a deal." He placed his hand in the small of her back and led her into the restaurant. The maître d' seated them at a corner table with a window view of the canal. It was perfect with candlelight and soft music playing in the background.

The waiter promptly appeared and filled their water glasses. He handed each of them a menu and Juan Carlos the wine list. He explained the chef's specialties and told them he would allow them a few minutes.

"Lacey, would you prefer an aperitif or drink before dinner?"

"No, thank you. If I drink anything other than wine, I will not make it through our meal awake."

He gave her that impish look again and she felt like she was reading his mind. She hoped the racing of her heartbeat was not loud enough to betray her thoughts. To fan the flames of heat rising from the pit of her stomach, she lifted her water glass and sipped. Then she took a deep, calming breath in an attempt to concentrate on the menu. Her mind was so not interested in food. Instead, she lifted her eyes and peered across the table. She committed to memory the arch of his cheekbones, the supple curve of his lips, long eyelashes that covered his eyes, a piece of curly hair that fell forward over his forehead. Wondering what it would be like to close her eyes and trace his features with her fingers. Embarrassed with what could have possibly gotten into her to think so intimately about a stranger, she decided it was time to fill the silence that stretched between them.

"Do you see anything you might like?"

He looked up from his menu with surprise as to what she might be offering. He knew she was not offering what he most wanted at this moment. "There appear to be many choices, but I will defer to the chef's selections. How about you?"

"Me too." Even though Lacey had no idea what they were. Who cared as long as she was sitting here at the mercy of this Adonis. It had to be a sin to look as handsome and sexy as him.

The waiter returned as she sipped water and fought to control her breathing. He explained the pre-fixed meal, the preferred wine selections to complement each course and the chocolate selection for dessert. She was not really paying attention until she heard the word chocolate. She asked the water to explain in more detail...warm flourless cake infused with melted chocolate and served with a mocha glace.

"Mmmm, that sounds heavenly."

Juan Carlos ordered for them, making mention that of course they would have chocolate for dessert. He selected the recommended wines. When the waiter departed from the table, he turned his attention back to his dinner guest.

"Lacey, please tell me about your fetish with chocolate."

"Why do you think I have one?" She challenged.

"Well, I met you admiring chocolates up close and personal in the shop today. And you were not the least bit interested in the menu until the waiter mentioned the word chocolate. Of course, you can correct me if I'm wrong in this instance, but I do not think I misunderstood.

She pondered her response as the wine steward came and poured. Once that was done, both glasses filled, she decided to jump in so as not to delay the inevitable.

"You are right. Chocolate is special to me. It is not a fetish, but like a lover of mine; a friend in good and bad times, never a disappointment and always available to satisfy whatever mood I'm in."

"You give chocolate an almost human status. Except that I'm hoping you do not consume human beings with the same passion as the chocolate." He gave her another one of his heart stopping smiles and she could see the amusement in his eyes.

"No I don't suppose I treat humanity in the same way."

"Well you were very kind to spend time with me today in the chocolate shop. Now upon hearing how important chocolate is to you, I am even more appreciative of the sacrifice you made in that shop."

Thinking it best not to get caught in his chocolate dipped honey trap, Lacey decided to ask her own question. "Juan Carlos, why did you give me the gift box of chocolates you picked out?"

"I wanted you to have it."

She captured her bottom lip between her teeth as her expression changed from carefree to serious. "But why?"

"Lacey, what I am about to tell you may be too much for you to hear, but I do not lie and I will not ever lie to you. I may not be forthcoming with information. However, if I am asked the right question, I tell the truth."

"Please tell me you are not a spy, sent to tail me. Not a stalker or psychopath" she lightly giggled. She averted her eyes and sipped the wine to calm her nerves. She was not sure what he was going to say, nevertheless some type of confession was coming.

"Go on."

"No, I am not a spy, stalker, or psychopath. I am a businessman totally consumed with work. I am here just until Monday and I do not know how to best occupy my time."

"I hope not to sound rude. But what does that have to do with me?"

"I was sitting at the café on the square trying to figure out my plans when I saw you standing in front of that shop. Next thing I knew I was on my way over. I wanted to meet you. Once inside, I could see you liked chocolates and I wanted you to explain them to me."

"What is there to explain. Some people just crave chocolates and I happen to be one of them."

"Well, I cannot wait to see you eat dessert."

As Lacey suspected time just seemed to pass easily in the company of this man. They talked about every meaningless topic as if it held some importance in their lives. There was no more mention of why they met or about his request to be his guide in Bruges. The waiter came by to clear the main course dishes and she realized the moment she had anticipated had come. Dessert!

When the masterfully arranged plates were placed before them, Juan Carlos noticed her eyes get bigger. She lightly picked up her spoon and ran her tongue across her lips. She carefully put the utensil into the center of the small cake and they both watched the hot lava of chocolate spill through. She then lifted the spoon to her mouth. Her lush lips parted and in went the piece of cake. She then turned the spoon in her mouth and licked every ounce of chocolate away. He wished he was about to run his tongue where the spoon had been. Her eyes closed at that moment and he inhaled the rich chocolate scent intermingled with her subtle perfume. He realized he had never seen anything so erotic in his life. He had a new appreciation for what she could do with a spoon.

Forgetting she was not alone, Lacey placed the spoon back on the plate. "That is amazing. It has been a long time since I had such a decadent chocolate cake as this."

"You make it look irresistible."

"Aren't you going to try some?" She asked as she drank the last of her wine.

"Yes, I think I will. Would you like some more wine."

"No thank you. I'm quite content to finish my dessert and savor every moment."

She lifted the spoon again and nodded that he too should partake. Following her example, he picked up his spoon and took a piece into his mouth. As she again licked her spoon, she found herself avidly watching for his reaction.

"Mmmm, this is very good. It melts in my mouth."

"I told you." She exclaimed,

To provide deference to every bit of chocolate, neither of them spoke. When the last little bit of cake was gone, she put her spoon down. She resisted the urge to scrape the sauce off the plate. Juan Carlos reached across the table and with his right thumb he rubbed the corner of her mouth, then placed it in his mouth. "You had a speck of chocolate left and I thought I would help you."

"Surely a napkin would have done the trick just as well." She blushed.

"Ah, but what pleasure is there in that? Now I have a priceless memory."

She eyed him suspiciously. "Juan Carlos, why do I feel like you are trying to seduce me?"

With amused eyes, he looked at her. "Maybe I am. Would that be so wrong? We are two adults with an undeniable attraction to each other."

"How can that be? We do not know one another."

"Si...yes. There are times in life when we cannot explain the why. It is true we do not know much about the other. Let's see if we can remedy that."

Unsure of the direction of his suggestion, Lacey started to fumble with her hands on her lap.

"Are you married Lacey?"

"No."

"Involved in a relationship?"

"No."

"Neither am I married or seeing anyone at present."

"Tell me what is your favorite thing to do?"

Lacey's face lit up. "My favorite thing to do is to eat chocolates from around the world. And yours?"

Juan Carlos did not hesitate in response. "Working with my executive team in the office."

"Where are you from?"

Lacey stiffened with that question. It brought memories back of her home with Maria. She did not want this to be a walk down memory lane with a man she did not know. "I am from a little town from the state of Virginia in the United States."
"Very nice. I figured you might be American or Canadian."

"Yes, I am definitely American" she chimed in. "Where do you hail from? I'd say Spain if I had to guess."

"Si, I am from Spain. I was born in a hospital in Madrid while my parents were visiting relatives, and our family home is on an estate just outside Jaen, Andalusia. My base of operations is Barcelona."

Lacey decided it was her turn to ask something of substance so she learned more about him. "Do you have brothers and sisters?"

"Yes, I am the oldest of six brothers. My brothers' names are: Tomas Miguel, Marcelo, Alberto, Leandro Cruz and Javier. We are very different in personalities, and dispersed throughout the world; yet we are very close."

With his response, she forgot she was supposed to be in command of the inquiry. She thought what it would have been like to have a big family. For as long as she could remember, it had just been her and Maria alone against the world. She was jarred from her thoughts by his voice.

"Do you have any siblings?"

"No, I am an only child."

"Do your parents find it worrisome that you are traveling alone so far away from home?"

With a veiled expression, she responded lightly. "No, they do not mind."

"Do you travel a lot?"

"No, this is my first trip in quite some time. However, I am always traveling the world in my mind or when reading a book. There are so many places to explore and so little time. I prefer to relax and get to know a place versus keeping up a frenzied pace." She paused as she realized she shared way too much in that response. "What about you, Juan Carlos?"

"I travel a great deal for work. I rarely get to see a place or soak up its culture."

"That is a sad commentary on life."

In a sexy purr, he responded. "Not at all. My work is important. I have many people who depend on me to make the right decisions. Unplanned sightseeing is just a distraction. Work is real and quantifiable."

Lacey wondered what made him so passionate about work. She had never really gotten into the joy of business. Until she quit to help Maria, she was a personal assistant. Working a nine-to-five left a lot to be desired in her mind. "If business is so all consuming to you, Juan Carlos, then why would you want to see Bruges through my eyes? We are so different."

"Ah, but this is planned sightseeing and as you may have glimpsed, I am not very good at relaxing."

Lacey laughed because he had so artfully compiled her words and used them to make his case. "Touché! You seem to be using my philosophy on travel to make the case that you need me or else you will have a miserable time here."

"Just speaking the truth."

She helplessly yawned. So as not to be rude she thought she should explain. She certainly was not bored, just exhausted. "Juan Carlos, as much fun as it is to banter back and forth as we 'get to know' one another, I find myself to be sleepy. I believe the effects of our jolt of chocolate are wearing off."

"I understand. Before you run off, please give me your decision. I hope I am not asking too much of you. I do enjoy your company, and I really want to explore Bruges versus being reminded that I am not at work. I think you know me well enough now to make an informed decision, si?" He paused and then spoke up again. "Plus, if you keep me busy in town, how can I possibly be idle enough to come up with creative ways to seduce you."

She noticed he had the most determined look. It was almost as if he was setting down a challenge or dare if she refused.

"Put like that, then how can I refuse. Yes, I will be your tour guide through Bruges."

"Excellent."

"Let's meet here for breakfast at eight tomorrow morning."

As she pulled back from the table, he stood up to assist her. She revealed her most defiant stance and held her chin at an angle. "Let's be clear I am only signing up as your tour guide for the next three days. I am not getting involved with you or going along with any plans for seduction. Goodnight." She turned and walked away.

As he watched her walk away, he sat back down. It was pointless for him to say anything or run behind her. He was starting to notice a pattern in Lacey's behavior. Who was she running from…him or herself? Her protest was little too breathy to believe she did not like him. The way she looked at him betrayed her words. She wanted him too. Great satisfaction swept through him. Picking up his wine glass, he imagined multiple ways to seal the deal. He smiled and quietly noted they had three days...*and tomorrow and tomorrow and tomorrow*!

Chapter 3

"A day without chocolate is a day without sunshine."
~ *Author Unknown*

In what had to still be the early hours before dawn, Lacey threw back the covers and sat on the edge of the bed. She felt like she had tossed and turned all night. She was at war with herself for wanting to act on her attraction to Juan Carlos despite the illogic of it all. He was in town for a weekend and she was not interested in a fling or a dead-end relationship. She wanted to be alone. She was exasperated. It was the same argument and the same results each time her mind drifted off to think of him. She was glad he found her attractive. Thus, she was comforted that she would not be the only one panting like a teenager when they were together.

"Ugh, I need exercise." A run through town in the brisk morning air was a perfect solution. A quick peek at the clock showed the time to be 5:22 am. If she went out now, she could run for forty-five minutes, come back, shower and be ready to meet him for breakfast.

At the front door of the hotel, she stretched and planned her route through town. Running against her own internal clock she had enough time to get in eight kilometres. There would be no distractions or diversions to her goal and off she went.

When she arrived back at the hotel she was refreshed and pleased with her time. She made the distance in forty-six minutes. Breezing through the lobby she picked up the *Brussels Daily News* and the *What to Do in Bruges This Week* flyer. She had never thought about what a tour guide did to prepare. However, it seemed simple enough to organize activities. She used to do that when she was employed full-time. Who knew how tightly packed Juan Carlos would want their daily schedule. Beggars can't be choosy…so she would do her best and he would have to accept it or leave her be. At least that is what she kept telling herself.

******

As the sun rose, Juan Carlos stared out the window looking across the horizon. He felt unsettled and wanted to burn nervous energy. He contemplated whether to take a run in the invigorating morning air or head for the gym and treadmill. He had already taken a cold shower to ease his aroused condition. So, he opted for the treadmill.

The resort's gym was not quite his state of the art facility back in Barcelona, but it would do. He

54

set his target incline rate a little steeper than his usual and switched on the television to the financial news channel. He began his regime watching the stock prices from the previous day. His mind strayed to thoughts of Lacey. He wondered if she was lying in bed asleep with that terry robe wrapped around her or if she was bold enough to sleep naked. He recalled her creamy smooth skin and the soft innocence she projected until pushed just over the edge. Once she reached the edge she gave back as good as she'd received. She was spunky. Amazing that he wanted her so much. He'd never had to chase any woman. They always seemed to be readily available when he wanted company. A quiet dinner that often ended in bed. Afterwards, he simply returned to his busy work life.

With Lacey though he felt different. He felt there was no hurry. It was so out of his normal character. He usually maintained a well-controlled patience and outwardly practiced coolness. His opponent rarely read his mind. While she what no business opponent, she was still an outsider. It did not feel that way. Around her he felt like he had all day to lounge. He wanted to tell her what he was thinking, how attractive and irresistible he found her. She was just being herself and that was enough. He wanted to make her happy so he could see her

smile.   When she said his name, he felt
vulnerable. If only she knew…

He did have one regret where she was concerned
and he planned to remedy it today. Life should
never be about regrets. He wanted to kiss her
pink lips and prove to himself they were soft and
supple.   It would take a great deal of inner
strength to pull away from that discovery if it
held true to his fantasy. He wondered which of
them would end the kiss first. It he was not
careful, Lacey would feel just how excited she
made him, and she might run for the hills.

Coming out of the daydream, Juan Carlos heard
a financial clip that mentioned his company and
the rumour of a deal close at hand for the
conglomerate's acquisition of the failing olive oil
manufacturing   firm,   Durante.   Gutiérrez
Enterprises was estimated at single-handedly
being able to save thousands of jobs; a move to
sure up the industry.   He stepped off the
treadmill, grabbed a towel and snapped open his
cell phone oblivious that it was early morning in
Barcelona.   He pressed the speed dial and
listened.

"Greg here" came the groggy voice on the other
end.

"Greg, I'm just watching the financial reports and I need an acquisition update."

"Juan Carlos, why are you really calling?"

"I want an update." He yelled into the phone.

In a patronizing voice, Greg said "I thought we all agreed no contact until the deal was closed."

"Greg, I did not agree to that. The Board made that arbitrary decision. Surely you cannot expect me to tune in to the news media to get updates on my own company."

"I would have called you if there was any pressing news and there is none."

"What do you mean? There was a news report on television so of course there is something to report."

"No, there is nothing new, so why don't you try to relax. It has not even been twenty-four hours since you departed. How is Bruges?"

Trying to calm his voice, Juan Carlos responded "I don't know how it is. I have not seen anything of the town. I am more interested in business." Juan Carlos knew he was stretching the truth a little, because while business was important, he had not solely occupied his thoughts with it since he arrived in Bruges.

"It is a new day, why don't you go out and explore. I am curious to hear what you find. Know there is no need for you to call me back today or even this weekend. GO enjoy yourself!"

"Greg, you are my dearest friend. I trust you would tell me if I should worry."

"Of course, I would, and haven't, so don't worry. Everything is going along as planned. We'll talk soon. Now go relax!"

With a grunt, Juan Carlos snapped the phone shut. A different kind of frustration crept into his body. He did not know how to adjust to not getting his way. The business needed him and he needed it. He switched off the television, got back on the treadmill and finished his run.

******

Smartly dressed and sitting in the atrium restaurant, Lacey patiently awaited Juan Carlos. She was purposefully early and had already sampled two different types of herbal tea and cocoa infused truffles she had brought down from the stash in her room. Today was a new day! The hours since her run had given her time to compose a tentative schedule. She still had yet to work out Juan Carlos' preferences. He would have to tell her if he required a midday siesta after lunch. Lacey always admired the concept of siesta and spending time devoted to family. The thought brought back memories of her travels with Maria through the small towns of Spain. One would be hard pressed to try to find an open shop during the siesta hours there.

Lacey doubted Juan Carlos would make time for siesta daily since he was consumed with work. If he did she wondered if he would nap in an easy chair or stretch out across a sofa. Would he lay across the bed with his secretary and have his own interlude? Would he suggest he and Lacey siesta together? Wow, what was driving these personal and intimate thoughts? She needed to stop this path of thinking. She was no expert and had little experience with men. In all her years, she had only a couple of short relationships which held no passion and seemed one sided. One thing she was sure of is that Juan Carlos did not need any help seducing her—he was doing just fine on his own.

"Lacey, am I interrupting?"

"Huh," she looked up. "Oh, Buenos Dias Juan Carlos; I was occupied planning our tour schedule."

He slid easily into the chair across the small table from her. His leg briefly touched hers and she felt his immediate warmth as he filled the small space. He was dressed in khaki trousers and a crisp dark blue shirt. The colour of the shirt intensified the icy blue depth of his eyes. She was spellbound by his eyes which gave one the impression they were as vast as the ocean. Again, she was lost to time and space.

Juan Carlos cleared his throat and with hesitation he saw Lacey come out of her own daze. "Lacey, you appear to be preoccupied this morning."

If only you knew. "Not at all; just not sure of your preferences. Remember I've never been tour leader before. Do you require a siesta today? I am able to revise our time to accommodate one if need be."

He smiled reassuringly, reached across and covered her hand with his. "No siesta is necessary. And I want you to stop worrying. When it comes to free time, I am not hard to please!"

"I'll make a note of that."

The server appeared carrying a carafe of coffee and asked if they would prefer the buffet or the menu. They both agreed to the buffet and coffee. Lacey thought it ironic how they had similar food preferences even though they were from totally different worlds. She had never actually seen him crave chocolate like her, but he did enjoy last night's dessert. Would wonders never cease?

With light and jovial conversation over breakfast they discussed the day's agenda. Lacey did not catch any glimpse of Juan Carlos trying to seduce her. Who was she kidding? Every time he spoke in his thick Spanish accent he was seducing her.

She explained they would take a walking tour as it is the best way to see Bruges and soak up its rich culture. It would entail monuments, museums and architecture to tell its history.

"Our first stop will be the famous Historical Museum Belfry and Halles, where we will climb up the 366 steps to view the city. Then I have a surprise stop for you. After that we will have lunch in a small café and continue our tour this afternoon at the Lace Centre. Our tour will conclude for the day later this afternoon at one of

the newest museums, the Frietmuseum—
dedicated to Belgian fries."

"It seems as if you planned our time so that I am
able to maximize all there is to see. Your
surprise sounds intriguing. I like it."

"There is too much here to see in one day or in
many days. I just want you to sample a few of
Bruges' jewels and maybe you will return again
to see more. I will save tomorrow's tour details
until we return to the hotel after the
Frietmuseum. Then we will be done for today."
Little did Lacey know he had no intention of
them parting so early.

They left the hotel together and started their
exploration of Bruges. Lacey was relishing the
fact that she was getting ready to see Bruges
through a fresh perspective. It had been many
years since she had last gone to the tourist places
in any organized manner.

She fixed her eyes upon him. In the bright
sunlight, she found herself lost in their glow.
"To start, I must tell you that Bruges is
considered the Venice of the North. As you
might have seen, it sits on many beautiful canals.
Strolling along them in this quiet Medieval city
is said to be very romantic."

"Would you consider it as such?"

Lacey's cheeks reddened at his question. "To be honest, I have never been here with a man. You will be the first male that has explored this city with me."

"When we are finished with our tour, I want you to tell me if you felt the pull of romance." He gave her an amused look that underlined his promise she would have enough information to determine if Bruges was romantic.

How was it possible that she thought he was no longer interested in her? Ha! As they turned the corner onto the cobble stoned main square near the Bellfry Tower, Lacey knew she was in way over her head...

Chapter 4

"Death by Chocolate – feeling strangled, suffocated
without having a tiny morsel of his lips back on hers..."
~ Anonymous

At the bottom of the vast stairway that led to the Belfry, Juan Carlos paid the entry fee for both of them. As they began their assent step-by-step up the curved staircase, Lacey led him into the tower. She told of the history of the building and they talked about the carillon bells. He was noticeably distracted by the sway of her hips as she moved ahead of him. *Mi Dios, she had luscious curves.* He grabbed tighter hold of the twisted rope that served to keep them on the path as they moved higher and higher. For some reason, there was no other traffic on the staircase. If he chose to pull her back in his arms would someone come along and interrupt?

At the very top they were treated to a breathtaking view of the Bruges skyline, including all the beautiful rooftops. In every direction one could see medieval structures, churches and gabled houses. Lacey leaned over the edge and pointed down to the cobble stoned streets below.

"Look over there. Because it is such a clear day, you can see the sea."

Juan Carlos walked up behind her and came within inches of touching all of her. She felt his breath on her neck. If she moved one centimeter back her body would rub up against his strong chest. She inhaled unsure what to do next.

"Lacey, this is a spectacular view."

"Well worth the climb to the top don't you think?"

He reached his hands out on both sides of her to clutch the tower wall. Then he murmured in her ear "I definitely agree."

In a nervous and squeaky voice, she heard herself say "if we wait here another five minutes or so, the bells will chime."

"I'm not planning to go anywhere."

Lacey half turned and caught the smoky look in his eyes. Before she could respond, she felt his lips on hers in an urgent kiss that ignited a fire of passion she could feel down to her toes. Gently he turned her body around and pressed her close to him. She instinctively put her hands on his chest and felt the strong muscles beneath. Oh, how she melted into his arms as if she could not get close enough. Her hands pushed up and wrapped around his neck. Divino!

Juan Carlos slipped his left hand up her back. As he felt her move into the perfect space made for her body, he deepened their kiss. She tasted of chocolate and had such soft, inviting lips. It felt too good to stop, and she was giving herself to him. Oh, if he did not stop soon, he would pull her down on the ground and take her right here for anyone to stumble across. He had more control than that. He was a man, not some lustful schoolboy. He wanted her legs curled around him with not a care for who could see them or any other sane thought. With regret, he tore his lips from hers. He softly kissed her forehead and gave her a hug. With that embrace, he wanted to convey the message this was not the end.

With stabbing disappointment and a cold shiver from the loss of warmth, Lacey smiled up at Juan Carlos. "I've never been kissed like that. It was quite pleasant." She blushed.

He smiled back at her. "Woman do not tempt me to do it again or else you and I will end up exposed to all of Bruges."

"Right." She turned her back to him and tried to calm herself. She had to get control of her emotions. That kiss had been phenomenal. It stirred feelings in her she had never known to exist.

While she stared across the sun glazed horizon in silence with his body lightly grazing her back, the bells started to chime. He took his arms and gently rested them around her waist. He whispered in her ear. "Lacey, querida, let's just take a few minutes to listen to the beautiful music before we move on."

"Mmmm okay. Therefore, I brought you here…for music with a view."

Alone together they listened in silence. To Lacey it felt they were the only people in the world being serenaded. When the music ended, Juan Carlos moved his arms to capture her right hand in his. He rubbed his thumb across her palm. It was an intimate touch she felt travel up her arm and down into the lower length of her body. The shiver that went through her was almost uncontrollable.

With an amused expression, he said "I would race you to the bottom of the tower, but that idea does not exactly seem safe."

She giggled out loud with a school teacher's warning but a girl's happiness. "I think we should practice some restraint as we have so much more to see and the hospital is not on our list for today." There was a glow emanating from her golden eyes as she scolded him for his idea.

"Very true. I think you have a surprise for me next. I definitely hope it is not the hospital or any building that once tended to the sickly."

"How could I forget? Our next stop is one of my favorite places in the whole wide world. Let's go." She pulled him to the stairway and he could not help but turn to momentarily look back at the view and the place where they shared what he believed to be the first of many memorable kisses. While he was not normally a nostalgic type, her enthusiasm was driving him insane. They descended the staircase a lot slower than their assent as they were content to share the same space and time.

Back on the street, Juan Carlos immediately reached for her and pulled her to his side. Now that he had found she fit perfectly next to him, he was not going to let her pull away. As they walked along, he reached over to gently tame an errant curl that had escaped her clip. "So where to next?"

"Just be patient and I will lead you there."

"But I want to know."

"Sometimes you have to relinquish control and trust your guide to take care of the details."

"Are you saying that I should just shut up?"

"That's the purpose of a surprise. I guess you are used to being in total control? Used to making all the decisions?"

"I have been told that on a few occasions."

"Well not today. You wanted me to take you where I thought you should go. So, let me do that. Now no more questions or interrogations. Details are not negotiable so stop trying to pry them out of me. We will be there soon enough."

Reaching into her shoulder bag she offered him first choice of the chocolates she held in the small box. Juan Carlos chose the praline flavored truffle and she selected an amaretto. She desperately hoped it had a real infusion of liquor to give her the courage to lead this man.

Idly walking along, they made small talk on the busy streets. Many townspeople were going about their day to work and school. Tourists really had nowhere to be until they arrived at the next destination.

"Many people here ride bicycles," he pointed out.

"Yes, thousands choose it. This town is eco-friendly and its natives are very much interested in preserving their way of life. The first time I came here over twenty years ago, one rarely saw a car. Crossing the drawbridge into the town exposed me to a secret world."

Curious to know more, he asked "who first brought you to Bruges."

Lacey smiled. "My grandmother, Maria. It was one of her most favored places."

"I can see why. It is not consumed by big corporate business and people who have little or no time to enjoy the simplicities of life."

"Juan Carlos, each day you choose that kind of life. Yet you seem to be lamenting it at the same time."

"I was not speaking of myself. I have many responsibilities and yes, every day I chose to lead a corporation. Everyone is not as driven as me. Yet they still prefer to be a prisoner to work."

Lacey stopped and stared into his eyes to see if she could make out happiness or sadness in his statement. There was no emotion there. Pushing the envelope, she said "maybe their leader is the one who has set the standard and they feel compelled to follow or else."

Juan Carlos felt as if her words were directed at him. Insulted, he opened his mouth to respond and then closed it as he recalled the reason why he happened to be in Bruges on hiatus.

"I have rendered you speechless. Wow." She could not contain her amusement as she looked away. She noticed where they were. "No matter, as we have arrived at our next tour stop: the Chocolate Museum. Here we will explore the history of chocolates, including the ones from here in Belgium too."

Totally consumed with how she switched subjects even when he did not want to, he conceded that they had indeed arrived in front of a museum. "They have a museum dedicated to chocolate?"

"Yes, and in case you were at all worried, we get to sample too."

Clapping his hands like a child to feed into her joy he laughed. "Oh goody, goodies!" All he could think about was how chocolate would taste as he kissed and plundered her mouth. He was going to find out. Ready, set, go. He pulled Lacey closer and ushered her inside.

The museum encompassed three levels of displays and a store. As they slowly strolled through the museum, Lacey outlined the history of chocolate from the earliest days into the present. He was aware of a few details he brought with him into the museum. Never did he feel as interested as he was listening to Lacey tell him the tidbits of information she believed he might want to know. Because it was a Friday in the off season, there were not many others sharing their tour. And true to her word, she ended their tour in front of a makeshift kitchen where chefs were busy demonstrating the secrets of chocolate.

"Here we will find our *piece de resistance*…samples of fresh made chocolate! It is the perfect culmination to end our tour." She giggled.

"Lacey, do you know how to make chocolates like the chefs?"

"Nope." She giggled again with her infectious laughter. "I rarely step into a kitchen unless it is to be an appreciative eater."

"I would definitely say you are more than that. At the very least, you are a connoisseur."

"Thank you, Juan Carlos. That is a compliment I wholeheartedly appreciate."

The chef held up the tray of samples and both Lacey and Juan Carlos selected pieces of interest. Milling through a corner of the shop eating samples, he pulled her into his embrace. "Did you know there was a time in history when the Church considered the consumption of chocolate an aphrodisiac, and thus banned eating it?"

Off kilter being held in his arms, Lacey thought about his question. When she opened her mouth to respond, he kissed her. He immediately ran the tip of his tongue along her lips and she melted into his arms, into his kiss. She could taste the flavors of their chocolate choices intermingling to produce a fiery and passionate response. How perfect. Her body was warming up all over with an urgent need to be satisfied.

Yes, yes, yes, yes....no, no, no—this was a bad idea. As much as it pained her, Lacey knew she had to put a stop to this kiss. There was something irresistible about Juan Carlos, and she loved being around him more than she thought wise. She was already gambling against destiny that she would not get hurt when their weekend ended in two more short days. She tore her lips from his and with every ounce of courage she had, she asked "why do you keep kissing me?"

"Querida, I cannot resist acting on my desire to taste you…especially this time. I wanted to taste chocolate mixed into your sweetness."

She felt the blush rise from her neck up into her face. She put the last sample into her mouth trying to ignore his response. Watching her chew, he admitted he was confused by her actions and decided to question her. "Do you not like the way I kiss?"

"Yes. No. I mean you are an expert kisser, but you and I should not be kissing." Ugh, why had she started this conversation?

"Given the chance to do it again, I am certain I would make the same choice. Our attraction is natural and I will not pretend it does not exist, querida."

Anger rose from deep within her. She was not sure it was his fault, but her own betrayal.

Indignant she looked him straight in the eye. "Well next time maybe you should ask me first before you just go and kiss me."

"It would be foolish of me to make such a promise. However, I will make a conscious effort to respect your wishes."

"Alright, let's continue our tour. It's time for lunch."

The rest of the day one tour passed quickly. After lunch, they explored the bobbin lace making heritage made famous in Bruges. Lacey mentioned her grandmother named her as a reminder of lace making here. Their final stop was the Frietmuseum, housed in one of the oldest building in the city. Lacey explained potato fries originated in Belgium, as did this museum—the first and only 'fries museum' in the world. Juan Carlos admired the building's architecture as they moved along each floor. At the end of tour, they were banished to the basement cellar. There they sampled tasty fries and sauces. All in all, Lacey believed the day had gone well. Juan Carlos seemed to have enjoyed their time together and the tour highlights she crafted.

As they leisurely walked back toward the hotel. silence ensued. Lacey could not believe it, but she was lamenting that their time today was ending. It had been an active but exciting day. The highlights for her were the two times Juan Carlos had kissed her. She could kick herself for telling him not to kiss her again. Her response was an attempt to protect herself from the emotions welling up inside; and it made perfect sense at the time. She was tense and knew she wanted many more kisses from him. She wanted him.

"Lacey, where did you go?" He had stopped to look at her.

In confusion, she looked at him. "Huh? Nowhere. I am right here."

"No, your mind left me. Do you find my company boring?"

"Not at all. I guess I was trying to decide what part of the day was my favorite."

He brushed his thumb against her cheek and tucked a loose curl behind her ear. "You are so kind to take this time to see this place with me. Every minute had been special to me."

"It was my pleasure. There are places I've seen today that I had never seen or taken for granted in the past."

"What shall we do now? It is still early."

"Aren't you tired of my company after nonstop activity since this morning?"

"Never querida. How about we find a chocolate shop and replenish your stash?"

"Really, you want to find one?"

"Yes, are there others than the ones we've been to yesterday and today?"

"Oh yeah, there are at least forty shops in this small town. All the major producers are sold here: Godiva, Hans Burie, Neuhas, Guylian, Galler and more."

Juan Carlos wove his fingers through her right hand and smiled down at her. "Take me somewhere new. Make your choice and I will happily go."

"Okay, follow me." She put a little more pep in her step and off they went.

An hour later with new boxes of hand-picked chocolates in hand they headed back toward their hotel. Lacey laughed out loud. "I cannot believe our shopping and tasting spree held the attention of everyone in the store."

"We were quite a sight. People passing by as we fed each other. They thought we are lovers. What a great thought" he said intently looking down at her.

"Well one thing's for sure, the shopkeeper was all smiles as we spent over sixty euro."

"Yes, a whole day's worth of sales in a few moments!"

"It's a shame one cannot eat chocolate alone. Real food is a must have too, but chocolate is a necessity."

"Lacey, don't you fear one day you might not like chocolate anymore?"

"Ha, perish the thought! Not at all. I've been eating it for so many years there is no way that could happen. Chocolate is like the water that one needs to survive."

"You know, you are the epitome of chocolate. Forever more when I think of chocolate, I will think of you."

Lacey was conflicted over what that meant, but thrilled at the thought that she would 'forever' be remembered by him. "That is the nicest thing anyone has ever said to me."

They walked along without saying anything for a while. When they were near the Landhuis, Lacey decided it was time to fill in the silence. "Tomorrow we will meet at 9:30 am. Our day will be themed history and architecture. For good measure, I will add a couple of historical churches so you have an almost complete picture of this area."

"Lacey, if I keep my promise not to kiss you and I keep my hands to myself, would you again dine with me this evening?"

"I don't think that is a wise idea. We've had a full day and I just want to turn in early tonight."

"How unfortunate for me. If you change your mind, you know where to find me."

"Yes, that I do. Thank you for a lovely day."

"It is I who is most grateful." It appeared to her that Juan Carlos' eyes moved down to her mouth and then back up to find her eyes. It felt like he was going to lower his head and kiss her. She was holding her breath in hopes he would break his promise and kiss her again. Instead, he slightly bowed his head and body toward hers. "Buenas noches, Lacey." Then he turned and walked away. She felt immediate disappointment, but had no one else to blame other than herself. This was how she had changed the rules of the game. All he was doing was abiding by her decision. How admirable. Now she felt rejected.

******

Juan Carlos slammed his hotel suite door shut. Why did he just walk away from Lacey? Damn her rules. He'd almost kissed her again in the lobby. He wanted to be kissing her right now; holding her in his arms and feeding her more chocolates. He plopped down on the loveseat and his head fell into his hands. What had he done wrong? He was taking it slow and they seemed to get along well. She pulled away from him and physically shut down. Was dinner too much to ask even with the promise it had pained him to make not to kiss her again. Just being in her presence without touching was better than nothing.

He got up and walked over the bar. He selected a glass and filled it with ice. Reaching for and grasping the scotch decanter he sighed. He put the decanter down. Alcohol was not the answer.

He pulled out a bottle of water and poured it over the sparkling cubes. Being angry solved nothing. Just because Lacey stood up to him was no reason to be out of control. He knew he needed to reign in his arrogance and see it for what it was. He was disappointed that she was not spending the evening with him. They still had all day tomorrow and Sunday. He felt she was fighting their attraction for one another. He reminded himself whatever was meant to be would be.

Could he take the chance that what he was feeling for her would be enough to leave to fate? Playing with the ice cubes in his glass, he moved to the window and looked out on the setting sun. He sensed he was still out of control. He needed someone to talk over these bizarre feelings. He put his glass down and picked up his cell phone. He would call his younger brother Javier. Javier is the most conservative of all the Gutiérrez clan. Javier listening and offering practical feedback was exactly what would fix this situation.

After a couple of rings Juan Carlos heard the connection. "Javier, how goes life?" Juan Carlos hoped his over-the-top happy mood would go unnoticed.

"Uh oh, what's wrong Juan Carlos?"

"Why does something have to be wrong for me to call?"

"Come now dear brother, I've known you all my life. If you call me and start the conversation about me, something is wrong. When it is about business, you barely let me say hello before you move into the corporate realm."

Exasperated, Juan Carlos sighed. "Okay fine, you win. I do need some advice."

"Shoot bro, I'm all ears."

"I met a woman yesterday and I think she's the one."

Javier hesitated a moment longer than usual. "What do you mean 'the one.'

With a deep sigh, Juan Carlos ran his hand through his hair. "I think she's the one I'm destined to be with...to marry, have babies and live happily ever after."

"Whoa, slow down. Start from the beginning. This does not sound like you."

Ignoring Javier's comments, Juan Carlos continued to talk as if he were talking to himself. "Is it possible to meet a person and instantly fall in love. Our meeting one another was so accidental. But now I feel like I need her constantly by my side. When she's not with me, I do not know how to occupy myself. I think of nothing else, but her."

"Juan Carlos, was the sex that good?"

"What?"

Javier felt he needed to clarify his comment. "Obviously if you are talking this way she must be amazing in bed. I've never heard you talk about a woman in this manner. Work occupies all your time and except for family occasions, nothing gets in the way of work."

"I haven't even slept with Lacey. We just kissed for the first time today. I can't let her go or get her off my mind. She makes me feel things I've never felt."

Javier listened until Juan Carlos stopped clamoring on about this Lacey. When there was silence on the other end of the line he decided, it was his turn to speak up. "How's work?"

"Javier, are you listening to me?"

"Yes of course. I asked you an important question. How is work Juan Carlos?"

"Work is fine. I'm away for the weekend. That's how I met Lacey."

"What? You are away on business and you let a woman distract you?"

"No, I'm on vacation for a few days."

"Something is not quite adding up. You don't go on vacation unless it's to come home for the family." Juan Carlos did not respond.

"Where are you Juan Carlos?"

"Relax brother. There is nothing sneaky or suspicious going on. I am in a little town in Belgium, called Bruges. Why are you interrogating me anyway?"

"Remember you called me for advice. I am simply trying to understand the entire picture before I provide my opinion."

"Fine. The Board sent me on a short hiatus. Greg thought I might like it here in Bruges." Juan Carlos filled in the rest of the details of his last couple of days. He left out the stuff he though too personal. As Juan Carlos finished his story, he braced for Javier's commentary.

"Well bro, that's quite some story and from what you said and didn't say, it only seems for now you are right in the middle of seeing how it will play out. I have a couple more questions and then I will render my free advice."

"Go ahead." Juan Carlos held his breath unsure he would like the questions.

"Do you feel this way because you cannot have her or because she is one of a few people alive who dare to challenge you?"

"I don't know why I feel this way. She does challenge me. But she also talks to me like I am a person. She does not see a corporation or make me decide how to proceed."

"Juan Carlos, either you are burned out at work and need lots of unplanned recreation or you have fallen in love. Maybe both. For a long time, your life has been too serious and required you to sacrifice everything to work. Now that you have been forced to think about other things, you've momentarily let your guard down. You are going to have to explore your feelings more closely."

"Go on, I know there's more."

"To be fair, it may not matter to her if you've fallen in love. You cannot make her want you or act on your mutual attraction for each other. She does not sound like the mistress type. My last word of advice to you is don't reach out to her if you do not plan to make the necessary lifestyle sacrifices to be with her."

"Thanks Javier, you make life sound so glum."

"Not at all. Love is a beautiful thing even for you older folks."

"I am not old. Thirty-six is a prime age to settle down."

"Whatever you say man. I'm still in shock you are even contemplating the idea. This is so out of character for you. If this woman is really leading you to make a serious commitment to something other than work, I cannot wait to meet her. You've met your match. Good luck. And Juan Carlos?"

"What now?" Juan Carlos felt his brother's smile through the line.

"Keep me posted."

"Yeah sure." As Juan Carlos hung up the phone he saw the last glimpses of the sun fall below the horizon. He would figure all this out. In the meantime, he had one more phone call to make.

On the opposite end of the hotel, Lacey sat huddled in the window seat. She had showered and was back encased in the warmth of the terry cloth robe. While the days are fairly warm, nights turned chilly once the sun descended. The fireplace had been lit as part of the turn down service. This hotel was a favorite as no desire went unfulfilled. Fireplaces, soft music playing, fluffy terry bath robes in every suite. More special were the two chocolate truffles elegantly boxed and left on your pillow each evening. It was the perfect complement to end the day. Looking out over the shimmering dark water of the canal, she still contemplated what to do about dinner. She did not have the strength to get dressed and each time she gazed across the room toward the room service menu her mind wandered back through the day's events. Juan Carlos consumed her thoughts. She needed a few moments alone to rebuild the chinks of her armor before morning. In reality, she was experiencing deep emotional loss. She missed him.

A soft knock came from the door. Lacey's heart fluttered. Could it be that Juan Carlos had ignored her request and come to collect her for dinner? Was it to be déjà vu like last night? She leapt across the room and peeked out the peephole. It was not him, but someone from the hotel staff. With disappointment, she opened the door.

"Room service for Madame." In wheeled a cart.

Lacey frowned as she looked down at the cart of food. "There must be some mistake. I did not order anything." The waiter set up the table for one in the sitting room. Lacey did not know what to do. Everything smelled delicious and she really did not want to turn it away.

"Also madam, I have one more delivery item for you." He went to the door and disappeared into the hallway. When he returned into the room, he carried a large vase full of mixed white flowers. Lacey gasped. "They're beautiful, but they can't be for me."

"Yes Madame, they are for you. There is a card. When you are finished with dinner, you may put the table in the hallway and we will come along and collect it. Have a nice evening and goodnight." He bowed, turned and left her suite.

Lacey was left standing there speechless. She stared after the young man as he closed her suite doors. She was not sure what to do next. She was immediately drawn to the floral bouquet and the card that sat atop the arrangement. As she reached out she felt her hands shaking. It could only be from Juan Carlos. No man had ever sent her flowers before.

Turning the envelope over in her hand she pulled out the card. It read: "A woman still has to eat. I miss you, but I do understand. Buen Apetito, Bon Appetite, Enjoy! Until tomorrow." It was signed simply, Juan Carlos.

She held the card to her heart and leaned forward to inhale the scent of her flowers. With a cheesy grin, she sighed. "He misses me too." At just that moment her stomach rumbled and she laughed aloud. "Perfect timing Juan Carlos, as I am starving." She thought to herself she was starving in more ways than one. No truer words were spoken. On that note, she turned toward the small dinner table and lifted the tops of several what looked to be tapas dishes. Small plates of traditional food from Juan Carlos' homeland. One held potato omelet, another stewed chicken in wine sauce, and another, sautéed asparagus. She could imagine him eating similar dishes in his room right now and immediately felt closer to him.

The last plate she uncovered held dessert—dark chocolate covered strawberries. Lacey was never one to embrace the rules so she picked up a strawberry and began the last course early. Licking the juice from her fingers she decided on a club soda, selected a glass and poured the fizzy drink into it. After one sip, she felt exotic bubbles enhancing the delectable flavor of chocolate and sweet fruit. Then she turned her focus back to the main dishes. She ate everything.

With a full tummy capped off with the last strawberry, Lacey gave into a yawn. She was totally satisfied or at least as much as she was going to be tonight. The thought sent a spark of heat down her body. It was time for bed. Rising from the table, she made her way to the bedroom. She climbed in between the soft covers with memories of the wonderful day gone by and the promise of a new one to come. What would tomorrow hold? She wondered wherever and whatever he was doing. She hoped Juan Carlos was thinking of her and the time they would spend together tomorrow. Maybe there was no harm in just one more kiss. After all she did owe him a proper thank you for that amazing meal and his thoughtfulness. Plus, she reasoned, she made her own rules and could to stretch them a little so as not to be rude. With that last thought she drifted off to sleep.

Chapter 5

"There's more to life than chocolate, but not right now."
~ Anonymous

Lacey walked through the lobby and sat down in the sitting area near the restaurant. After another restless night, she was fit to be tied. She did not even want a big breakfast today or even chocolate. All she wanted was a kiss from Juan Carlos. Definitely not normal for her. She jumped up and started pacing. She could not think of a way to get him to kiss her again. She did not plan to beg, nor did she have any intention of having a discussion. One simple kiss was all it would be so he would know how thoughtful she believed his dinner gift.

"Lacey, why are you out here? I thought we were going to meet for breakfast in the restaurant." Juan Carlos searched her face looking for the answer to his question.

Why did he always catch her in some daydream, Lacey thought. Not sure how much to say, she hedged her answer. "Yes, well I wasn't hungry after such a big dinner. I thought maybe you were still full too."

He smiled. "I don't usually eat breakfast so I was merely going to eat to be polite. And who knows when you will feed me, so better to be safe than..."

Lacey stretched her head up and placed her lips tentatively on his cutting him off midsentence. She felt him stiffen while he tried to register exactly what was happening. She captured his lower lip and then rubbed her tongue across his upper lip. As she kissed him, she inhaled his scent. He smelled of expensive aftershave and with the last bit of resistance seeping away, she leaned her body into his.

He deepened the kiss, caught her body in his arms, pulled her close while matching her enthusiasm. It was as if time stood still. No one and nothing else mattered.

Struggling for sanity, Juan Carlos put her away from him. "What happened? One minute we were talking about food and in the next you are kissing me."

Lacey shyly looked away. "I wanted to thank you for last night. I figured a kiss might suffice. Was I wrong?"

"Woman, you are driving me insane. One minute you are saying no kisses and the next you are kissing me. Not that I'm complaining but I would like to understand what you want."

"I'm sorry to be confusing you. You make me feel out of my element. I was impressed with how kind and sensitive you are to me when you do not have to go out of your way. I don't know. Wait, I thought you enjoyed kissing me!"

"I do." Juan Carlos ran his hand back through his hair. "But you are not ready to freely kiss me. Something is holding you back. I see it, but don't know what it is. I want more of you when we kiss. You feel it too, and then you put it back on a shelf as if it never existed. I'm just a man Lacey. I am far from perfect, and you are testing my limits."

"I don't mean to do that. I don't want you to think of me as a tease. It's just...." She turned away. "I don't know what I'm doing. I don't know."

Juan Carlos came up behind her and put his arms around her. "Lacey, it's okay. I did not mean to push you for answers you do not have. Let's start our tour early. How about we pick up some chocolate croissants from a street vendor as we walk along?"

Turning into his embrace, she said "chocolate sounds heavenly right now. Are you sure you do not want to stay here for breakfast? Remember this may be your last chance to eat today." She smiled and breathed a sigh of relief. Juan Carlos had given her an escape route for the moment and she gladly took the lifeline.

He looked down into her sparkling eyes. "Positive. Where to now?"

Lacey laughed," chocolate first, then City Hall."

Letting her go, Juan Carlos said, "ah, a woman who knows the finer things in life."

They walked out of the hotel briefly chatting about the day ahead. It was a warm autumn day and the sun was high in the sky. The first stop was a street vendor who sold them croissants and coffee. They resumed an easy pace strolling through the cobblestone streets as they ate. They visited the Government Palace, College of Europe, new concert hall, and the historical museum. They saw Dutch and Belgian paintings at the famous Goeninge museum, and passed by a statue of the town hero, poet Guido Gezelle.

Exhausted with culture, they stopped for lunch at a sidewalk café. They munched on sandwiches and frites. In the afternoon, they explored Bruges most renowned churches, the Basilica of the Holy Blood and the Church of Our Lady. In the later, they saw Michelangelo's small marble statue of the Madonna with Child. Lacey explained the significance of the artifact—it is supposed to be the only known piece of its kind that ever left Italy while he was still alive.

When they were leaving the Church, they saw a wedding party coming into the building. They stopped to gawk at the fanfare. Lacey whispered "Bruges is a very popular place to get married. You know that romance thing I mentioned the other day."

Juan Carlos leaned over and whispered back. "Do you fantasize about being a bride on your wedding day? What would you wear? What it would be like to be married?"

Lacey said, "no! Stop talking about happily ever after. It doesn't exist."

"Says who?" He retorted back at her. "It exists for my parents who've been married for almost 40 years. It existed for your parents. You should allow yourself to believe in it."

Not wanting to talk about her situation, she flipped the questions back on him. "What about you Juan Carlos? You believe in marriage, yet you still aren't settled down and married. Why is that?"

Her questions sobered him. "Marriage always seemed like a tomorrow kind of idea. I think I was awaiting the right woman to show up. Someone I will love and adore. I will one day have the kind of bond my parents share. It will last until death separates us."

Agitated that he could think of another woman in her presence, Lacey needed to say something to shift the conversation. "Speaking of the wedding theme, our last stop today is the Diamond Museum."

They walked along in silence. Juan Carlos realized with Lacey he was dealing with a master at changing subjects when the topic did not suit her. He knew she was hiding something that would explain her vehement objection to happily ever after. Had someone hurt her enough to make her unwilling to dream as all women did about being swept off their feet by Prince Charming and living out their fairy tale. She was practical and unwilling to take risks. Why? That question had plagued his mind all night. It kept him from knocking on her door when he was unable to sleep.

After paying the entry fee at the Diamond Museum, they walked in holding hands. It would seem that whenever he reached out their hands naturally found one another. As Juan

Carlos walked around listening to facts he already knew about the diamond as a stone and industrial material, his mind was elsewhere. He held Lacey's slender left hand in his and imagined what type of diamond ring might inspire her to give her heart to him. He relished the moments spent with her and the sparkle of her amber burning eyes watching him, tentative and curious of his movements. How was he ever going to resist temptation for one more day when that was the last thing he wanted? How could he idly sit on the sidelines and let her escape from what they might have together. That was not his style. He always played to win. Yet there was a frailty in Lacey beneath her tough exterior. There was more to know and he was going to find out. He hoped with every fiber in his body it was not a showstopper for what could be between them. After all, he had fallen in love with her from the moment he first saw her.

Admittedly he knew so little about her life—how she grew up, what kind of career she has, what are her deepest goals and aspirations for life, how she would bring about world peace—all an undiscovered mystery. As he watched her from veiled eyes he recognized he had experienced her on a deeper level. Her favorite treat was anything chocolate, her most enjoyable memories took place here in Bruges with her grandmother, she is named after bobbin lace making, loves chocolate truffles and traveling, changes the subject as an avoidance tactic, is kind and caring, takes time out to help others, is a great tour guide, kisses passionately, feels good in his arms, stirs his desire to a feverish level, has beautiful diamond faceted eyes that darken when she's turned on. A shift in his body brought him back. He was aroused in the middle of the museum. His muse was talking about something. So as not to embarrass them he reigned in his own desire.

In a sober moment that was more important than desire, he acknowledged his commitment to her. All these traits, and so many more he had yet to name, sealed his destiny. He loved her and wanted to spend his life keeping her happy. He would buy her chocolates every day. She could take chocolate bubble baths. He would rub mocha chocolate lotions and oils into her skin. He would lave chocolate ice cream across her stomach and lick it off inch by inch.

Lacey stopped and looked at him. He was somewhere else. Maybe he was so focused on business he did not hear her question. "Juan Carlos?"

"Si...yes," he said switching to English and answering guiltily as he knew she was aware he was not paying attention. He ran his hand across his face trying to focus.

"I asked if you minded that we missed the diamond polishing demonstration. It happened at 12:15 while we were at lunch. If you really want to see it, we can make a stopover here tomorrow."

"No, no. I do not need to see it in person. The exhibits show it well enough for me."

"Very well, are you ready for our last adventure on today's schedule?" she asked. "It is just a short walk away."

Juan Carlos nodded and placed his hand in the small of her back. He felt instant warmth electrifying through him as he touched her.

They left the museum and walked along the edge of a canal. There was a slight breeze blowing and the curls in Lacey's hair gently stirred in the wind. All the while, the sun provided an angelic glow to her face. All Juan Carlos wanted was to kiss her again, and see if below that angelic demeanor was a vixen awaiting his masterful touch. He was quickly losing control of his body as every thought ended up with them in the same place, his bed. Grasping at anything that might lighten the mood, he said "Lacey, may I have a chocolate?"

Frowning she thought about his request. "I don't have any chocolates with me. I completely forgot to drop the box in my bag this morning. I would really love to have some."

A look of concern came over his face. "Do we have time to find a chocolate shop before our next adventure?"

Lacey spoke in her sassiest voice, "there is always time for chocolate. In a few minutes, I'm sure we will pass by a chocolatier. What do you fancy right now?"

Knowing that the purr in her voice was meant to be about chocolate, he could not resist an opportunity to tease her. With a devious smile, he said "stop asking questions you don't want answers to?

Lacey laughed. "You know I meant what kind of chocolates do you want."

"I want chocolate hazelnut," he said. "How about you, Lacey?"

Stopping in the middle of the block, she paused. "Hmmm that's a tough choice. If I were eating dessert, I would want a crème caramel drizzled with rich, dark chocolate sauce." She spun around to take in all the directions. "Look, there's a shop over there. It just might have a crème caramel hidden beneath a dark chocolate. If not, I will settle for *'anything chocolate.'* Let's go find out!"

Juan Carlos reached out and touched her chin to turn her attention back to him. He smiled down at her and asked "is anything chocolate a flavor?"

Lacey gently rested her hand on his forearm. "Of course not silly. I was noting that I will happily substitute for my choice if they do not have what I said I wanted."

"I won't Lacey," he said. "I never settle for second best in life."

Not sure if they were still or had ever been talking about chocolate, and not wanting to know, Lacey turned her attention back in the direction of the shop. "Well I guess it's a good thing every chocolatier has hazelnut flavors."

Juan Carlos laughed heartily. "I hope you are right. Let's go find out." Off they went in the direction of a group of small shops edging the canal. Hand in hand, they crossed the pedestrian path dodging a few bicyclers hastily riding along with somewhere to be. Juan Carlos realized that neither of them had any care in the world at that moment other than acquiring chocolates as priority number one. He was sure for the moment he was going to have to temper his desires to have Lacey in his bed until Lacey freely gave herself up to him. Short moments later they emerged from the chocolate shop holding hands and another box of hand selected divine sweet treats.

Lacey thought at this rate she would be way over weight before the weekend ended. Eating this much chocolate was not good for her figure, but the temptation was too much for her to resist. If she was going to be successful at keeping Juan Carlos at arm's length, she needed to depend on chocolates for strength. Chocolate had seen her through every major crisis in her life. While this encounter with Juan Carlos was a pleasant weekend distraction, she teetered on the edge of a crisis. If she gave in to the passion they obviously both felt, she would be left to pick up the pieces when he went back home in two days. Sharing chocolate with a man was almost too much for her. The intimacy they shared made her blush and the way his lips caressed and devoured the hazelnut crème truffle almost undid her self-control. He was so handsome with his dark features and come hither presence. She hoped he did not notice the way she had watched him in the store. To calm herself, she combed the whole shop to no avail in finding her flavor. The substitute she selected was tasty—a simple chocolate caramel. Who was she trying to fool, any chocolate was a great flavor, and at any time.

Lacey looked up and noticed that there were almost to their next destination. In sight was the final touch she planned for their afternoon, a cruise around Bruges by its canals. Such an intricate and delicate balance of land and water created the illusion that trade still depended on one's ability to move their wares from place to place. It was these waterways, well preserved and treasured, that provided much of the romance to the lovers who found themselves here in this quaint village town.

She looked up and smiled. "Juan Carlos, here we are for our boat ride."

He looked down into her shining eyes. "Wow, I never thought about taking a boat ride along the canal. It is the tourist thing to do. After you."

With the assistance of the crew, they stepped aboard. She thought to herself, for the next half hour, there would be no interference from the outside world. They could share whatever they wanted. Oh, maybe that idea was an over dramatization as their boat would make numerous passenger pickup stops along the way. Since it was the off season, there might be smaller crowds trying to board. These canals were not the Seine River, nor was their vessel a Bateau Mouche, the famous boats that sailed through Paris. Instead, they would be treated to a more intimate and serene ride to gaze up at local architecture in close quarters. The ambient light of sunset sparkled on the water as they listened to facts being shared about Bruges.

Juan Carlos slipped his arm around Lacey's shoulder and she leaned into his warmth. Her dress had slipped above her knee. He then placed his free hand on her leg. At his touch, they both looked down, and she felt her breath catch.

In Spanish, he said "relax, bella." Heeding his advice, she eased herself back against him to enjoy the moment. It was another perfect ending to their day. She felt the beat of his heat that left her more aware of him. The trace of cologne mixed with his earthy scent sent chills up her body. She closed her eyes and imagined what it would be like for him to belong to her. What would it be like to awake each day wrapped in his embrace, to hear his endearments, to feel the touch of his sleek hands caressing her smooth skin, to watch his blue-eyed gaze darken just before…"*Mmm*"

He whispered in her ear. "My, my, my, Lacey, what are you thinking?"

Panicking, she stilled. Had she spoken aloud. Her inner voice of reason was screaming "*you are betraying us. Not good!*" She flushed. "I was thinking aloud. We've had such a lovely day. Another great one here in Bruges."

Juan Carlos smiled down at her. "Yes, perfect." He lifted his hand off her leg, took her hand and wove his fingers through hers. Her leg felt the immediate loss of his hand on her flesh. Nervous and unsure of herself, she spoke in a voice barely above a whisper. "Juan Carlos, would it be too much to ask of you if you might kiss me here and now?" She bit her lip trying to figure out how much to say. "I find myself wanting one of your kisses. I mean sometimes the way you look at me makes me feel so desired. Am I imagining it?" She noticed she was rambling on, talking more to herself than to him. "You are a lot like chocolate to me. If I have a little, I want more. Kissing you leaves me insatiable. I don't know. I just…"

Juan Carlos lowered his head and captured Lacey's mouth in his before she could utter one more word. He could see her struggling to come to grips with what was happening and he wanted to assure her he was right there feeling the same amazing connection with her as she was experiencing. It was a tender kiss, yet far from innocent. She gently placed her hand on his chest, feeling his heartbeat and the core of his strength bulging through his shirt. He thoroughly kissed her as to leave no doubt that he could go on kissing her forever. The gentle rocking motion of the boat kept her tightly sealed in his embrace. Pulling his lips off hers first, he kissed her forehead, and then whispered in her ear. "Lacey, you never have to ask me for a kiss. I will supply it without you having to provide an explanation or ask a question. It is my pleasure to join my lips to yours. I imagine the many places my lips would like to discover on your body. Just know though that you have a dramatic effect on me. I am sure you understand being that we are in close proximity to each other at present. I will not take advantage of you or move any further unless by your command."

In a daze, she just nodded her assent to his statement. The kiss they shared was the most romantic thing that had ever happened to her. Not wanting these few moments to end she simply laid her head on his chest and watched the boat captain maneuver them along. While she sat silent her mind was racing. It would be so easy to let this weekend get out of control. It was already out of control! Contrary to what she thought she wanted, she now knew she wanted more. No, she needed more. In a couple of days this man had successfully gotten past her radar and all her defense mechanisms. She had fallen in love with him. Taking a deep, calming breath she silently said I love him. The same inner voice that kept coming along now whispered to her: *now what are you going to do!* Worry crept into conscious mind. What was she going to do? That nagging voice failed to respond. How convenient! This little revelation would have a dramatic impact on her life. She had never been in love, but she knew as sure as day that she loved Juan Carlos. What were the options? She could ignore her feelings and check out of the hotel without him knowing it. She would never have to see him again and he would not find her. They could both return to their lives none the wiser. That option did not sit well with Lacey. The thought of never seeing him again was unsettling. However, that was exactly what will happen on Monday anyway. They will walk away. Juan Carlos will have memories of this town and she will have memories of him. The way he is holding her right now, the seal of his lips on hers, the unique masculine scent of skin, and his strong presence – who would've imagined that. Anything this memorable happening to her was not an ordinary occurrence.

All she planned was to be an expert chocolate critic for her own personal joy.

You have options. Options! Lacey went back to assessing her options: she can let this weekend play out like it was supposed to. She believed one cannot change fate anyway. They had met, grown to know each other. Wishing it was any other way was pointless. What harm would it be in being romanced for another day. If she was right that she loved him, then she was going to be heartbroken if she ran now or gracefully made it through the rest of the tour. One thing was for sure, she would not totally give herself to him. She couldn't risk it feeling like he abandoned her as everyone else always did. Without thinking, Lacey reached into the box of chocolates on her lap and popped one into her mouth. Life was good this minute. She was wrapped in the arms of the most scrumptious man and eating life's best food offering. Everything was right in her world for now...

All too soon their canal voyage returned through its loop and it was time to depart. Juan Carlos moved his arms to allow Lacey to get up first. Moving deafly next to her, he gently handed her off to the crewman so she could return to the bank. He moved up to stand next to her.

"So, what do you think of Bruges by boat?"

"So far, it has been my favorite part of our tour. Having time to unwind and hold you in my arms was priceless."

Lacey's face reddened. "You say the nicest things to me. Are you trying to make me blush?"

"Not at all! I just call it the way I see it."

"Yet you noticed I am blushing."

"Yes, truth be told, I like to see you blush, and I like having you in my arms." Payback is fair play. He smiled and pulled her into his arms.

"Yes, it is," she said as she held onto him for dear life.

As they hugged, he asked "will you do me a favor?"

"I'm listening, even though I'm not sure I won't live to regret it."

"Have dinner with me?"

She sighed. "I thought we decided yesterday dinner is not a good idea for us."

"No, Lacey if I remember correctly you decided that. Look, it does not matter. Yesterday's gone. Tomorrow may never come. Let's focus on the here and now. Have dinner with me?"

"So poetic Juan Carlos!" She huffed as she walked out of his embrace.

Frustrated, Juan Carlos ran his hands through his hair. "Lacey, it's just dinner in a public place with no strings attached. We have to eat." His words implored her to listen. He was compelling to her sense of reason. She could not afford to skip meals.

"I don't know. I've eaten so many chocolates and have not made time to run. If we have dinner, it will derail my plans to exercise."

"Is that the only reason Lacey? So you will not miss out on exercising? "

"Yes, today that is the only obstacle." She lied, but it was better to lie then to knowingly put herself in a dangerous position. She did not fear him. She feared her own reaction when she was around him. Already she had chattered on and on about her feelings exposing too much of herself. If she had an intimate dinner with him tonight, what else might slip out? She was not willing to find out.

"Okay then, I will amend my requests. The sun has set. And the lights of the town are coming on. Let's head back to the hotel, get changed and go for an evening run together."

"Huh? You want to run with me?" Lacey inner voice piped up again: *'let's see how you wiggle out of this one Missy!'*

"That's right, we'll table the dinner idea and go for a run. Running is my favorite way to blow off steam and burn calories."

Feeling defeated and outsmarted at her own game, Lacey said, "all right you win this time. We'll go for a run."

"It'll be fun, you'll see."

"Yeah, lots of fun." She sounded unconvinced. At least she would burn off some of the chocolate she was about to eat as she reached in the box for consolation.

Juan Carlos asked for details on their way back, deferring to her to choose a path that was well lit. Not that he was at all worried they would run into anyone to bother them, but he was desperately trying to calm her nervousness. He liked the way she wore her emotions outwardly even when he was aware she was hiding so much more beneath the surface. It would be so good when she trusted him enough to be totally open.

Back at the hotel when they parted in the lobby, they had already established they would meet back up in twenty minutes. As part of his warm-up, he ran up the stairs two at a time to reach his room floor. For two days, he had anxiously tried to get her to leave the hotel with him at night. He would much rather have taken her to his suite and made love until the sun came up. The next best thing was a romantic run through the lit streets of Bruges. He would have to be extra careful not to get distracted by the curvaceous sway of her hips or else he may lead them into a canal.

Twenty minutes went by quickly. They met clothed in athletic gear where they had designated to meet. Juan Carlos was appreciative of the tight-fitting leggings that Lacey had chosen to wear. He fixed his eyes on her and his thoughts were sinful. Good thing they were headed out into the lower temperatures as he could feel his body warming up. Any minute now and he would start sweating without exerting himself. Moving ahead in the lobby, he took her hand and pulled her out into the street.

He asked "do you need to stretch?"

"Nope, I already did so before I came downstairs. How about you?"

"Done, let's go!" He turned in their agreed-upon direction and began their sprint. Lacey followed catching up easily. She knew he was purposefully controlling his pace as his legs were much longer than hers.

Their run lasted about an hour. They slowed their speed on the way back. Passing through the main square, Lacey realized she had really enjoyed the run. She felt exhilarated. And hungry. Matter fact, she was ravenous. What harm would there be in mentioning that she was hungry to Juan Carlos? Her inner voice spoke up: '*I wouldn't use that exact phrase if I were you!)*' Duh, you are me!

"Juan Carlos, do you want to grab a quick meal at an informal place here in the square," she said. He stopped to look back at her.

"You're hungry? Great because I just realized I'm starving."

They moved toward a neon sign that read Crêperie. Lacey envisioned herself polishing off a chocolate banana crêpe. With that thought, went all the value of her run in one quick step.

This man was a bad influence. Not really! She would've chosen the same thing even if he had not been with her. They sat down at a window seat, and ate their hot crêpes. Hers was drizzled with chocolate and his was a ham and cheese. When done, they walked back to the Landhuis Hotel. Just inside the door, Juan Carlos found her hand and pulled her close to him.

"Lacey, thank you for going on that run with me. You are a strong runner. I had to stay on my toes out there in this foreign city which doesn't seem so foreign anymore. And, you made a way for us to share dinner. You never cease to amaze me!"

Impishly she said, "it was my pleasure. Know that you never have to ask me to go with you running. I willingly go as it is a great way to burn maximum calories so I can eat more chocolates."

Not to be undone, he said "I can think of other ways we can burn more calories."

"I'm sure! Good night Juan Carlos." She let his hand go.

"Buenos noches, mi querida." He reached over and gave her a quick hug. "Until tomorrow..."

"Yes, I have a surprise for you in the morning. Don't eat breakfast. We'll meet here at 8:00 AM."

"Si Senorita, yes ma'am. I will see you at 8:00 AM sharp."

He walked her over to the elevator and press the button for her. The doors open immediately and she boarded the lift. After the doors closed, he spun on his heel and headed toward the bar. He needed a drink and to be amongst people. If he had gone back to his room instead of the bar, then he already knew he would be having graphic thoughts of Lacey sprawled across his bed in those tight pants and the sports bra he felt beneath her jacket. Sighing, he ran his hands through his hair again. It was getting harder to let her leave him unfulfilled. He wanted to strip her of everything that she held back from him, touch her, and make no apologies for whatever happened between them. While it might seem going to the bar would be a distraction, who was he fooling. He spoke out loud, "Oh, yeah right! What a good night it is going to be…NOT!"

Chapter 6

*"A true chocolate lover finds ways to accommodate his
passion and make it work with his lifestyle..."*
~ *Julie Davis of the Los Angeles Times" (10/30/85)*

Coming out of the shower, Lacey felt refreshed.
Her run last night was just what the doctor
ordered. Remembering back, she had come
upstairs from Juan Carlos' embrace and headed
right into the shower. Letting the hot spray of
water drench every part of her body had released
all the worry and anxiety of the day. She slept
many hours and was glad she had set up a wake-
up call or else she might have overslept. Nothing
had changed overnight regarding her feelings for
Juan Carlos. She felt love for him as strong as
ever and she was still unsure what to do about it.
Time moved on despite one's indecision.

She walked over to the chest and selected
today's outfit, a blue long peasant skirt and white
loose fitting top. To combat the morning air, she
was sure would face them, she reached for her
wool wrap scarf. When the wind died down and
the sun was high in the sky, she could put the
throw in her canvas bag. She slipped her feet into
some low slides and popped a chocolate into her
mouth. All ready to go, she picked up her bag
and headed out of her suite to the elevator to take
her down to the lobby.

Juan Carlos watched Lacey cross from the lifts. He was captivated yet again by her beauty and the ease to which she changed her look. Today a simple clip held up her curls at her neck in a low ponytail. She appeared refreshed and ready for a new day. He saw none of the tiredness that had darkened her eyes when he had last held her in his arms. She was dressed like a carefree peasant with an oversized flowing skirt that hid her sexy legs. It was in direct contrast to the skintight cat suit she had on last evening. He likened her to a purring feline he would stroke until she curled around him with no desire to escape. Yes, that was an image he could endorse.

When she stopped in front of him, he resisted the urge to capture her in his arms and take her to his bed. The urge was getting stronger and he muttered under his breath in his native tongue. "Bella!"

"Good morning to you too," her eyes belying she heard him.

"Buenas Dias, beautiful!" He pulled her into his arms for a quick hug. When he let her go, he looked down into her eyes and he was smiling. "You caught me at a weak moment. Everything is better now!" He said those words to convince himself and he did not want to upset her.

She smiled as if she held the biggest secret and said "Are you ready?"

"Yes, and very curious about my next destination!" It was not like Lacey to not share their itinerary.

"Our chariot awaits, come!" She then held out her hand and as if she were a magnet, he was drawn to her.

Hand in hand they walked out the front of the hotel. At attention was a horse-drawn carriage and a coachman. The driver opened the door and stepped aside. He introduced himself as Captain Ben.

"After you!" Juan Carlos offered his hand to lift her into the velvet red carriage. Once she was seated, he lifted himself and sat next to her. Their legs brushed each other and his hand went around her shoulder. At the front of the carriage were two beautiful brown horses ready for the command that would whisk them down the lane.

Captain Ben held the reins and turned to stare at them. With a thick accent, he spoke, "Madame says you all have been touring for days, so I will spare you listening to me drone on about my hometown Bruges. Enjoy the sights and the quiet ride with Bessie, Matilda, and me. You will be just fine!"

Juan Carlos took the opportunity to pull Lacey closer so he could snuggle up next to her. After Captain Ben had returned to facing the street, he whispered to her. "This is a pleasant surprise. Almost a romantic gesture. It pleases me very much."

Giggling, Lacey turned slightly toward him. "Now Juan Carlos, you know better than that! I am not the least bit interested in creating romance. However, I thought it the perfect way for you to see the alms houses, cottages, windmills, bridges and more scenic views of Bruges on our way to brunch." She looked up at the sky as she bit her lip and said, "I hope it won't rain though with these overcast skies."

"Lacey, while you won't admit it, this ride is romantic! I won't complain as I enjoy having you in my arms until we arrive at some unknown location for a feast!"

Lacey cut her eyes toward him. "You are incorrigible!" He laughed and she leaned back to watch the scene unfold.

As the carriage journeyed along they thoroughly explored the quiet and equally busy streets. They saw people headed to church and to market. Bruges was a kaleidoscope of sights and sounds. All the while, Lacey lay comfortably in Juan Carlos's arms. She admitted to herself, it was a romantic setting. Her inner voice asked: '*so, you gonna tell him you think it's romantic?*' No way! And thank goodness, their destination was just up ahead.

Château Minnewater, the restaurant where they would have brunch sat facing the infamous *Lake of Love*. No tour of Bruges was complete without a stop there at the lake. When originally planning their itinerary, Lacey did not give this landmark a second thought. Now though she hoped she did not live to regret coming to see it with him. Juan Carlos made an ordinary walk down the street extraordinary. No doubt their time at the lake would be memorable.

Captain Ben pulled up along the walkway into the castle. Matilda and Bessie seemed ready to stop. Perhaps it was feeding time for them too. "We've arrived at Minnewater sir and m'lady." He jumped down and held the door open for them. Juan Carlos got out first and then helped Lacey down.

"It has been my pleasure to bring you lovers here for years. Enjoy your time."

"You mis…" She began speaking and Juan Carlos cut her off saying "Captain Ben, thanks for a great ride! It was a pleasure neither of us will ever forget, right querida?" He looked at Lacey with amused eyes that begged her not to try to explain their relationship. Even if she tried, he knew their actions spoke differently.

Lacey said, "yes, Captain Ben much thanks to you, Bessie and Matilda!"

Captain Ben said "well I've been around a long time and it does me good to see love blossom. You two have something many people crave, so treasure it always!"

Both Juan Carlos and Lacey were speechless. Captain Ben climbed back onto his carriage and drove away.

Lacey would not look at Juan Carlos. She was not sure she wanted to see what he was thinking. "That was interesting!"

Juan Carlos said "yes, that Captain Ben is quite a character."

She smiled. "I'm sure now, I will never forget this experience."

"Me either. Shall we go in?"

Lacey followed Juan Carlos inside the quaint setting. They were escorted to a table on the veranda overlooking the lake. Once seated, they were left alone to review the menu.

"Wow, this is spectacular!" He said as he looked out over the lake.

"Is this your first time seeing the lake!" She asked.

"Yes, I saw signs around town for Minnewater but did not know what it meant."

"This lake is the most traveled to spot in the whole area. And while it is a very couples oriented locale, I say everyone should see it at least once."

"I can see why," he said. "It is a very calming experience to watch the water."

"After we eat, would you like to walk around the lake?"

He smiled, and said "but of course!"

"Your wish is my command." With that statement, Lacey lowered her eyes pretending to study the menu. She already knew its contents as she had seen it before selecting this restaurant.

The waiter appeared with a complimentary bottle of champagne. Every weekend people flocked here to drink and be merry in this idyllic setting. This was shaping up to be the perfect day. Lacey was sure she would not forget any detail. As the waiter poured, she turned her head to look out over the lake. There were many swans floating along in the way the water shimmered even on this overcast day provided a sense of tranquility. She then turned Juan Carlos who briefly chatted with the waiter. He sensed she must've been looking at him, and asked the waiter for a few minutes while he focused his eyes on her. Her eyes trailed down to take in his open collared shirt unbuttoned just enough for her to see his bronze skin. He reached across the table for her hand. Lacey hesitated a second longer than necessary. He turned his hand palm side up, and took his eyes off hers to look down at his hand. She followed his gaze, then as if knowing he had her full attention he looked up into her eyes and said "Lacey, do I really have to ask?"

"No," she whispered and placed her hand in his. He gently stroked his thumb across her fingers while he watched her.

"Lacey, what do you want?"

"I don't know. What are my choices?" As she pretended she meant food, she broke their stare and looked back down at the menu on her lap. He continued to rub her hand and she was wildly distracted. Her heartbeat raced. Her inner voice threw in: '*you know what he means, tell them? Or are you really that afraid*?' Oh gosh, she needed some chocolate! Looking around, all she saw was the delicate champagne flute. With her free hand, Lacey picked it up and took a big gulp. She said "I'll have whatever you're having."

With the defeated sigh, Juan Carlos said, "all right Lacey, let's play it your way... For now!"

He summoned the waiter and ordered for both of them. He selected the homemade shrimp croquettes, salad, and powdered Belgian waffles served with a choice of syrup or chocolate sauce on the side. When the server departed, Juan Carlos turned his attention back to her.

"Lacey, tell me about growing up in America. What are your best memories in life?"

She pulled her hand back from his and put it on her lap. "Why do you want to know about life for a child in America?"

124

"I don't want to know about any child, I want to know about your childhood in America."

Juan Carlos could see a range of emotions playing across Lacey's face. If he guessed right, when she responded it would be to change the subject.

Stalling for time, Lacey did not answer. She turned her head again and looked out on the lake. She was thousand miles away. "I came here as a child."

Juan Carlos was right, she had changed the subject. He said "what did your parents tell you when they brought you here? Did they take you to the same places you've taken me?"

She stayed very still. He knew something was not adding up. "Lacey what is going on? You shut down and I don't know what to make of it."

Without turning her gaze from the lake, she quietly responded, "my parents died when I was a child."

"I'm sorry. I did not realize your parents were deceased. How did it happen?"

"I don't want to talk about it with someone I don't know!" She lied. She knew Juan Carlos in the most basic way a man and woman can know each other. She had given her heart to him and didn't want him to know it.

Without meaning to, he had boxed her into a corner. He needed to make amends and let her know that he was here for her. He said, "I do not mean to pry. If you ever want to talk about it, let me know."

"I apologize Juan Carlos, as I did not mean to sound harsh. I'm very much a loner so I'm not used to being questioned."

"I understand. Really, I do Lacey. I hope you will forgive me for being rude," and he smiled that heart stopping smile that he knew charmed the world.

They sat in awkward silence for the time it took their salads to be served.

In another attempt to make small talk, he looked for a safe subject. Juan Carlos asked, "what do you do for a living?"

"Not much. I was an executive assistant for a while. Now, I don't do anything anymore except eat chocolates. That's my desire, my escape!"

In a lighthearted tone, he said "really? So maybe your next career choice should be chocolate taste tester, or dessert critic specializing in chocolate."

She smiled. "Perhaps I will consider it. Do you think I'll be any good at it?"

"I have no doubt you will be good at anything you put your heart and energy into."

She hesitated. "It does sound like fun. But I don't know if I can be successful."

Sensing the mood shift, Juan Carlos said, "come now Lacey, how many languages do you speak?"

"Six, well if you count English, seven. I am fluent in French, Spanish, Latin, Dutch, Portuguese and Italian."

He was amazed. The woman sitting across from him had many hidden secrets. And he looked forward to unraveling them all. He said, "Lacey you are also well-versed in chocolate, a great tour guide, you travel the world fearlessly, and you are in excellent physical shape. Is there any doubt that you are and will continue to be successful at all you choose to accomplish?"

"I guess I never thought about it like that. I would love being a chocolate critic. I used to dream about opening my own chocolate shop. In each weekend, I'd host a chocolate tasting and anyone could come in and sample. There was a place when I was a child where the workers would sing while they made fudge. There was always a sample, and lots to buy. When I earned good grades in school, I would ask Maria to take me there." She paused not knowing where that memory came from, but it was a good one to have.

He said, "we rarely had chocolate when we were children. My parents thought it made already hyper and over active boys more erratic. Now I rarely deprive myself of anything I want to eat, including chocolate. Life is short!"

Lacey chuckled. "Well, you don't have to watch your figure."

"True, I'd much rather watch yours." And he smiled.

"Yes, now I see why your parents try to keep you from indulging in anything to make you more crazed!"

For the rest of the meal they made small talk. When the last plates were cleared, Juan Carlos reached for her hand for the first time since their meal began. "Let's go for a spin around the lake?"

Lacey gave him her hand. She also looked up at the overcast sky and back across to him. "Okay, if you think the rain will hold off until we return."

He took his gaze off her, and looked up at the sky. "It should, but I promise we will not melt with a little rainfall. Come!"

Chapter 7

"All I really need is love, but a little chocolate now and then doesn't hurt!"
~ Lucy Van Pelt (in Peanuts, by Charles M. Schulz)

Juan Carlos and Lacey slowly walked around the lake hand-in-hand. As they meandered along, they passed by couples in love out for Sunday stroll. Lacey admired the look of happiness in their eyes. Then she recognized the same feeling existed within herself. The little inner voice whispered: *'when was the last time you felt happy?'* It had been a long time coming. As they stood next to each other on the bridge looking at the famous Bruges swans glide across the water, she had thought about chocolate. She couldn't remember if she had eaten a chocolate swan since she had arrived in Bruges. Bruges had its own special chocolate, called the Bruges Swan. Strangely enough, she did not care at this moment whether she had eaten one or not... It would be easily rectified later.

Juan Carlos came to stand behind her, and whispered against her earlobe. "Thank you for the Sunday surprise!" He pulled her close so that her back touched his chest. Lacey nodded without turning around. This was the perfect moment to not move, and then it began to drizzle. Soft little drops fell to make puddles on the lake. The soft pelting of raindrops was so easy to watch.

"You know I'm glad you did not also ban me from holding you to close too. It would be even more impossible than not kissing you!"

"Ha, I can add it if need be," she joked. If she was being honest, she was not sure she could live without feeling his strength and warmth.

Juan Carlos debated with himself to say more. He was now in too deep with this woman to walk away. With that thought he was taken aback. Never shy in expressing himself, he was compelled to press on sharing how he felt. "Forbidding me to kiss you is quite enough!"

She spun around in a fiery blaze. "What do you mean?"

Letting her go and running his hands through his hair, he felt she was again building up her wall to block him out. Not this time. He said, "you put me on a shelf. You purposefully keep me at arms-length. What happened to you Lacey? Please tell me! Don't go through life like this!" He waved his hand through the air.

"Like what?" She felt overwhelmed and then said, "why do I have to have a story to tell? Why do you need to know my secrets, my innermost concerns? I shared my desires to escape, received a few hugs and kisses. Even felt inspired in your arms to share my love of chocolate. Is not that good enough?"

"No, Lacey it's not. I don't know what kind of relationship we started here. It was not my intention to get involved. But one thing I do know is you must live life abundantly. Tomorrow cannot hold regrets of what you failed to do yesterday. You cannot give up, or shut me out. You feel this too, the connection between the two of us. So, don't deny it with me, and at the very least don't lie to yourself."

"You are too self-assured, Juan Carlos!" She bit down on her bottom lip to stop from saying anymore. She felt the tears begin to form.

"I have to be and I will continue to be that way! I am true to myself and will not apologize for it. I go after what I want as I know if you let opportunity go by, it might not be there when you go back." He pulled her back into his arms and felt her resistance to believe in him. He rubbed his hands soothingly along her back. The first breakthrough in their standoff came when she laid her head on his shoulder. He whispered, "it's okay, I'm right here."

He heard her soft whimper as she began to cry. It tore him apart piece by piece to know he had started this here and now. He would not regret it, but it still did not make it easier to live through. He lifted her chin and with sincerity said, "I'm sorry Lacey, please don't cry."

Mother nature chose that moment for the skies over Bruges to open in a downpour. As sheets of rain poured down, they stood there on that bridge staring into the pools of depth that shined through their eyes. Thunder sounded and Juan Carlos came back to earth. He let her go, and took her hand as they began to run for shelter. Under an archway, they stopped to catch their breath and get re-oriented.

Lacey began to shiver from the cold. He could see she was drenched from head to tell. That was not acceptable. He pulled her to him, and rubbed his body against hers. When she stopped shivering, he rubbed his hands up her arms. He pushed her wet hair back off her face, and his hands found their way to cup her cheeks.

He gazed deeply into her eyes and said "Lacey, I can no longer resist my overwhelming need to put my lips on you. I want to taste you." He lowered his head and kissed her so passionately he felt the heat of their bodies mesh together.

Adversity left Lacey and she put her arms around his neck holding on for dear life. When he lifted his mouth from hers, they were oblivious that they were still soaked through. With the confidence to go after what he wanted, Juan Carlos said, "come siesta with me!"

She knew she heard him through the daze of arousal. "I'm sorry, what did you say?"

'Come siesta with me. I want you as I have never wanted anything in my life or anyone.'

The inner voice chimed in '*are you going to take a chance? It may be your last chance woman!*' Lacey was plagued with indecision…not about what she wanted to do or how to respond. Her confusion lay in what she would do after he let her go. Who would pick up the pieces of her broken life? Oh, did any of that really matter. She had to seize the moment. Juan Carlos was offering himself to her.

"Yes" she shook her head as she lifted her eyes to meet his gaze.

"Are you sure this is what you want? I need you to be sure."

"Yes, this is what I want more than anything, except maybe a morsel of chocolate." She nervously smiled and he knew she meant it. Her sincerity touched him to the depths of his soul. What a woman she was to step forward and accept what he was offering. He was aware she lacked the self-confidence to live as if she had not a care in the world. Admiration was too cliché to describe his emotions. He felt devotion and would bet his latest acquisition that she had no idea the impact she has on him. Soon enough he would show her just how much.

He pulled her back into his kiss. They stood there for quite some time. At some point, some semblance of rational thought entered into Juan Carlos' brain. "Querida, I do not want to stop, but this is not the place. Let us go back to our hotel. I want you in my bed now!"

The rain had let up to a light drizzle. Holding hands, Lacey led them down the path that would take them back to the Landhuis for an afternoon of passion. She liked that Juan Carlos did not mind if she sometimes took over. She had spent so much of her life making independent decisions. That was how she was raised. However, Maria was quick to point out: a woman needed to know that the man always leads, but the woman is always right. It was the gift of womanhood that showed one how to stand by a man and quietly offer wisdom so he would make good decisions. She did not need to take credit as he would adore her. That was enough.

Back at the hotel, Juan Carlos pulled Lacey close so there was no mistaking he had any intention of letting her go. He felt young again as he fumbled in his pocket for the key. There was so little keeping him from having his heart's desire ~ Lacey. Lacey shivered against him as they moved along. Just moments to go...

Arriving at his suite, he reached around her and pushed the key into the slot. The door clicked and he turned the handle. The brightness of light escaped through sheer curtains at the window. He ushered her in, shut and locked the door, and turned her to face him. Moving his arms up her back, he rested them on her shoulders. One hand cupped the back of her head and with the other he lifted her chin to place a tender kiss just next to her lips. Then he kissed the other side. 'Mine' he whispered. Then he lowered his head and kissed her. They both gasped for air as his hands found their way to her hips. He pushed her against the door and imprinted himself on her. She could smell the faint lemony scent of his aftershave in the air. All her molded to him through wet clothes. Her body was begging to escape so she could wrap herself around him, skin to skin.

Taking a step back, the hardest step he had ever taken, an idea surfaced in Juan Carlos' head. He took her hand and led her toward the ensuite bathroom.

"Juan Carlos, where are we going? I thought..."

"Shhh querida, don't you trust me?"

"Yes, but..."

He stopped and faced her. "Lacey, we have to get rid of these wet clothes and warm up. I will not have you get sick when we could have prevented it."

What he said made sense. Making love would wait. She gave up arguing and put herself in his hands.

Inside the bathroom, he left her side and turned on the shower full blast. Lacey felt she was watching a movie as an outsider. This was a surreal moment, one she had dreamed of often since meeting Juan Carlos. While she longed for this to happen, she never really believed Juan Carlos would ever make love to her.

Back at her side, he kissed her forehead, each eyelid, her neck. His hands softly touched her arms. Her eyes closed naturally and her heart raced as she enjoyed the seduction. Oh, my I could really get used to this! Then she felt his forefinger trace the edge of her shirt's bodice. She held her breath unsure if she would die right here in his care. How could a simple touch be so erotic? He unbuttoned her shirt and let it fall to the floor exposing her white lace bra.

"You are breathtaking" he said as he unhooked her bra freeing her to him.

As he kissed the trace of her neck down to the midpoint of her chest and tasted her breasts one by one, he said in a low voice, "I wanted to give you a bath, but I know I cannot wait that long to possess you. A shower will have to be good enough." No man had ever thought to tell her such things. No one compared to Juan Carlos.

He released the strings that held the skirt to her curvy hips and it fell to the tile as well. All that was left was her thong that matched the bra he had tossed away. Lacey felt Juan Carlos' hands touch the curves of her body and her head fell back. This feels so good. Never had anyone worshiped her body like this. He was paying homage to her as if she were a goddess. Lips caressing and lapping at her…it was just divine. Her nipples were erect as they pressed forward to be as close as possible to him. She was not just warm, but hot all over. If he touched her there she would burst from the excitement.

He knelt at her feet and pressed his head to her flat stomach. He held her as she stroked her hands through his black hair. With adept fingers, he pulled her underwear down over her hips. He kissed the center of her core, now exposed to him, where seconds ago, she had been hidden from view. He pressed his hands against her buttocks tightening his hold on her as he tasted her.

"Juan Carlos, por favor, please!" she moaned.

"Not yet, remember what I said. We must shower."

He then stood up. She watched him strip all his clothes away. Wow, he was an Adonis with toned muscles, dark hair, and chiseled masculinity. Together they made it across the hot, steamy misted room and walked into the shower.

Lacey felt she just needed to touch him. All of him. First, his chest. She played with the thick masses of hair. She smoothed it down as she felt his hard muscles tense beneath her touch. In a natural curiosity to see what he would do, she eagerly moved her palms down past his abs to caress him. He was so erect there was no denying she was turning him on. Lacey felt powerful knowing she could do this to a man as handsome as Juan Carlos. She reached out and gently grasped his naked hardness touching his slick, smooth skin. She barely had him in her hand when she heard his sharp intake.

"Lacey, if you touch me like this, then we will never make it to bed."

"Mmm and why is that a bad thing?' She heard him curse to himself.

"For one, if we make love here in the shower, we will possibly be creating a new life. I am a responsible man and I must make good choices even as you tempt me to take you now."

"Good point. I guess I was lost in the moment."

"It is a great thing to hear that you are lost in me. I feel overjoyed that you give yourself to me. To honor you, I will show restraint for both of us." With a warning look in his eyes, he said "as long as you do not touch me.'

Lacey felt disappointment seeping into her psyche because she really wanted to touch him with reckless abandon. Just being naked in the shower with a man seemed like reckless behavior. Lacey moved under the jet stream of hot water letting it wash over her hair and skin. Coming up behind her, Juan Carlos said, "Lacey it is my turn to take care of your needs, to pleasure you and ensure you never forget this day."

He reached up and selected pink shower gel. With his free hand, he put his arm around her waist and moved her back from the front of the shower. He then sat down on the marble shower bench and pulled her to sit across his lap. At the back of the shower stall the water flowed more slowly from this second stream of water. It was like a spring day's waterfall pouring out to provide relaxation and comfort.

Juan Carlos lathered up the soap in both hands and spread the rose scented foam over her body. He started with her pink, painted toes and moved slowly up her legs. With lustful eyes, he watched her squirm. Her movements as she sat upon him were almost too much. The more she wiggled in his lap, the harder he became. When he reached her thighs his hand purposefully skipped up her body. He laved her neck and shoulders with a slather of bubbles. She lifted her arms above her head and he spread soap from her fingertips down her arms and ended his exploration by caressing each of her breasts. Thankfully where the water washed away the soap, he replaced it with kisses. Holding her in his arms was heaven on earth, but he needed to move her to finish the washing.

With tense fingers, he adjusted her position so each of her legs was now over his, and her back was against his chest. With slick hands lathered and warm he placed one on each thigh just above her knee. In a thick, hoarse voice, she heard him say, "you tease me with the smoothness of your skin. When we were in the boat yesterday, I imagined what it would be like to put my hands right here and then slide them up."

With each inch, he slid his hand up her thigh, Lacey could feel spasms. When he reached the edge where her most delicate womanhood could be felt with his fingers, she was panting, "Juan Carlos, please don't stop."

"You want this Lacey? You want me to touch you here?" He touched her with his thumb, not needing to move his hands from where they held her thighs.

"Yes, and I want to feel you inside me."

"Mmm, si querida. And you will very soon." With his thumb, he stroked her until she could no longer hold back from orgasm. Not able to resist needing his kiss, Lacey turned, straddled him and kissed him on the lips.

"I am so hot right now, can our shower be done?"

"Yes, this is where our shower ends, but our pleasure continues." He lifted her. She wrapped her legs tightly around his waist, and her arms around his neck. He turned off the water and stepped through the glass door. He set her down, reached for a towel and dried her off. He then wrapped her in a terry cloth robe, dried himself and slung a towel loosely around his hips. Needing to be in close contact with her body, he lifted her in his arms and carried her from the bathroom.

Juan Carlos laid her down on the bed with a gentleness he did not feel. He had waited for this moment far too long, and he hoped he did not mess it up. Sitting next to her on the bed, he reached out and touched her face trailing his fingers down her cheek and across her lips. The softness of her skin was so different from his rough and calloused hands. She was such a contrast to who he is as a person. He knew he did not deserve her, but he had to have her. How would this work? How does one make time in their busy life to keep up a lifetime love affair? He was after all, just a businessman. Trying to figure out how they might mesh their lives together was overwhelming even to him.

Lacey turned her face into his hand and kissed his fingers and hand. All rational thought went out the window as she lifted herself to meet him halfway and pulled him down to her. As he leaned over her with his upper body their kiss deepened to a fevered pitch. Her mouth opened and their tongues met in a dance of lead and follow. Tearing himself away he whispered into her lips, "my, my, my Lacey...you are a temptress!" With massive curls spread across his pillow, he saw her half-closed eyes had turned to smoky amber in a look that said devour me. He brushed his hair back and tried to calm his breathing. The time had come to make good on his promise. She would be his. He reached into the nightstand drawer, pulled out a foil package, and with patience he clearly did not have, he removed the towel and sheathed himself.

Lacey watched with eager eyes as Juan Carlos removed his towel. There was a sheen to his body that glimmered in the shadows. There was no mistaking his hardness. True to his word he sought to protect her and her heart leapt more. He turned back to face Lacey and she saw raw lust in his eyes. Standing above her, he traced his right hand along the edge of her robe from her neck to the place where the two pieces of cloth joined above her breasts. She leaned into his hand wanting more than anything to feel all of him. He inhaled a deep breath and slowly let it go. "I have imagined opening the gift of you since I saw you that night. You are such a beauty that you should never be covered up in this robe or anything."

As he rubbed his hand just inside the folds of her robe, she sighed and looked up into his eyes. "I am not so experienced at this. I hope I do not disappoint you."

"That is not possible. Just give yourself to me, as I will to you and we will reach ecstasy together."

She nodded her head in agreement. He untied the robe and pushed it open. She heard him speaking in Spanish, but could not make out what he said. He then laid his full nakedness across her body with his legs gently separating hers. Their bodies fit perfectly. Lips met again and they were kissing with passion. He moved his hands to experience all her lush curves while she rubbed her hands down his rock hard, muscled body. Her touch sent shivers down his spine. Pressing against him were breasts that deserved his attention. He trailed kisses from her lips down her neck and to her nipples. It was hard to choose between each breast, so he lavished both with equal attention. Taking turns sucking and gently biting one as he rubbed the other with his hand. Under him Lacey was rubbing herself against him and he was losing concentration. He moaned. All he wanted was to be surrounded by her warmth. Returning to kiss her swollen lips, he simultaneously used his hands to spread her legs and he pushed inside her. 'My Lacey.' With enthusiasm, she wrapped her legs around him giving him more access to heighten the feelings when he thrust into her again and again. As the pace brought them closer to the edge, she could feel his muscles tightening. Lacey was losing all control as she felt waves of pleasure rock her body. Juan Carlos lifted her chin and stared into her eyes. "My precious Lacey we come together?" She nodded. With one last thrust they released themselves to a life-changing orgasm. They both knew nothing between them would ever be the same again.

With a light kiss to her lips, he moved off her, pulled her to his side, and wrapped his arms possessively around her. "That was perfect" she said as she laid her head on his chest and brushed a kiss across his damp chest.

"Si, querida."

Just holding her was enough to make him want to bury himself inside her again. He ran his hand across the wild curls of her untamed hair. Knowing they both needed rest, making love again could wait. He contented himself with gently rubbing her back as they both fell asleep.

Chapter 8

"Giving chocolate to others is an intimate form of communication, a sharing of deep, dark secrets."
~ *Milton Zelman, publisher of "Chocolate News"*

It was the same…always the same. She was being held back and they would not listen. She screamed again and again. "Take me, please take me. I want to go with you. I belong with you. No, please don't leave me!" And they always left her. She felt the tears stinging her eyes as she thrashed from side to side. She cried out in agony "let me go," as she begged release from whoever held her. When she had no more fight in her she fell to her knees and wept. She felt herself being picked up and gently shaken. Something was not right. No one was ever there to help ease her pain.

Her panicked screams woke Juan Carlos out of his lazy slumber. Lacey was in obvious distress. He had heard enough to know she was begging someone to take her with him, and she had to be restrained so as not to follow. She was fighting to escape his embrace. His first instinct was to be jealous of whoever commanded so much longing from her soul that she would beg not to be left behind. Then common sense said to him this was more than unrequited love. "Lacey, is everything alright? I'm right here." He held her tightly and felt her resistance disappear. "Lacey, wake up! No one's going to hurt you. It was just a bad dream."

The word dream brought Lacey back to reality. Where was she? She opened her eyes and looked into the concerned eyes of Juan Carlos. He held her in his strong, protective embrace. Lacey felt safe…for the first time in who knows how long, she felt like everything would work out.

Wiping away the tears from her stained cheeks, he asked "Lacey, what were you dreaming?"

Lacey felt like a rag doll spent of all her energy. "It is nothing. Just a dream I sometimes have when I'm really exhausted."

"You seemed to believe it was real while you slept. Please tell me. I will not let anyone hurt you, so there is nothing to fear."

With no resistance left, Lacey sighed. "I dream about my parents dying. It seems as if I am just a little girl again. It takes me back to the night of the storm, and I scream after them to take me home with them." She filled him in on all the details of that night, and the years since. She did not feel like hiding secrets from Juan Carlos any longer. He cared enough to have patience with

149

her and understood that she had a past filled with pain. He kissed and caressed away all her woes. When she finished her tearless story, he made love to her slowly and thoroughly. She felt complete.

Hours later they lay snuggled up in bed watching sunset over Bruges from the open curtains. There was a half-eaten box of chocolates next to them on the bed.

"Thank you for a memorable day." She leaned over and whispered into Juan Carlos' ear.

Holding her close he responded "I think we worked well together today. We both made it special. Thus, there is no reason to thank me. But if you want to reward me with more of you, I shan't complain."

Lacey knew he was right. They had both given of themselves all day long. She smiled. "Want another chocolate?"

"No more! I need a hearty meal. I've worked up such an appetite."

She shrugged. "That leaves more chocolates for me! I don't want to get out of bed." She rubbed her body against his and intertwined her legs with his. "Do you really want to get up and go out?"

He groaned. "Woman, at this rate we will never make it out of bed!"

"And you'll starve!" Lacey tried to keep a straight face. He rolled over so he was on top of her.

"No I won't. I'm going to have you."

She laughed. Lacey could feel he was all ready to go again. "Well I guess I can't let you starve." They made love and this time it was hot with passion. They found themselves all over the bed.

Sated from their afternoon of passion, they lay next to each other in the bed. Lacey appreciated Juan Carlos's creativity. She was aching in places she did not know existed. And now she did have to admit she was hungry. As if hearing this thought, her stomach growled in agreement. "Juan Carlos, while your caresses feel wonderful, it would seem that my stomach wants more."

"Oh, now you're hungry for food too!"

"Yes, but I still do not want to get up. Can we order room service?"

"Your wish is my command." He rose from the bed and disappeared into the other room. He came back holding the room service menu. They both figured out what they wanted, he ordered, then he climbed back into bed next to her.

Lacey thought it was best to start a conversation or else they would end up missing dinner altogether. She said, "Juan Carlos, I've shown you Bruges. Now you tell me about your home."

"You want me to tell you about Barcelona?"

"Yes. I hear it is beautiful and very cosmopolitan."

He proceeded to tell her about the city, its culture, captivating views of the Mediterranean, and the life he carved out there. He could even see himself as her tour guide when she came to visit. Lacey was so beautiful and she would outshine the best that Barcelona and all Spain had to offer.

Not too long after that, dinner arrived and they talked throughout their four-course meal. Lacey felt as if she would burst from the happiness coursing through her. With a full stomach and the sexiest man alive sprawled out next to her, she did not want for anything. Well maybe that's not true. At this moment, all she wanted to do was sleep. Sensing the vibe, she was giving off, Juan Carlos got up, turned on soft music and turned out the lights.

"Buenas noches querida" he said as he climbed into bed and pulled her into his arms.

"Good night and sweet dreams!" He gave her a kiss on the lips and held her close. Lacey put her arm across his chest and lay her head on his shoulder. She listened to his breathing while the music played and matched her pattern to his. In true comfort, she fell asleep.

Chapter 9

"After eating chocolate, you feel godlike, as though you
can conquer enemies, lead armies, entice lovers."
~Emily Luchetti

The phone was ringing. But where was it? Juan Carlos could hear his cell phone ringing in the distance. He looked over at the alarm clock. It was after 9:00 AM. Sometime in the night, he and Lacey had made love again. As he was on holiday and in bed with Lacey, there was no need to set the clock. He knew they could get up whenever they wanted to not at all.

The phone kept ringing. Who could be calling? He eased quietly out of the bed so as not to wake her. He found the phone on the desk in the sitting room. The caller identification showed it was Greg. The last thing Juan Carlos wanted to do was talk business. He turned off the phone. Whatever Greg wanted could wait! He wanted to be with Lacey when she woke up. So, he set the phone back down and went back to bed.

Not long after Juan Carlos had gone back to bed, the hotel phone rang. Stifling a curse, Juan Carlos picked up the phone. "Now is not a good time." He did not listen to who was on the line. After he made his statement, he hung up. Greg should get his message loud and clear and stop calling.

Lacey rolled over and said, "someone must really need your attention!"

He could see the teasing glint in her eyes and the slow grin that played across her face. "Si querida, you do!" He kissed her and forgot all about the interruption from the phone.

When they finally broke their kiss, Lacey frowned. "Juan Carlos if you need some time to return phone calls I'll understand."

"Lacey, are you tired of me already?"

"No way! I just know you are very busy executive. Surely they must need to consult you on some decision."

"It can wait!"

"Don't you have to return to Barcelona today?" She could not hide the disappointed feeling after voicing the words.

"No, I don't have to go back today. I can extend my holiday at will. We can explore more of Bruges!"

Lacey was silent and was biting her lip. Then she spoke, "I have no other places on our itinerary to show you."

"We can always spend another day in bed!" The thought of making love all day with her was extremely appealing. He hoped she would agree. His desire for her only seem to be growing the more he touched her.

"No, we cannot spend our whole day in bed!"

Like a wolf who had his prey lured in a trap, he said "then I have to make the most of our time now!" And they did.

Chapter 10

"Do you dream in chocolate" – Lindt Chocolatier

Just before noon, Lacey convinced Juan Carlos that they needed to get up and have some semblance of a day. They agreed to shower, dress and meet downstairs to have lunch. As soon as she left his room to return to hers to dress, he felt the loss of her. It amazed him how much he had come to depend on being in her presence. The sooner he was ready to go, the sooner he could meet her in the lobby.

He was in the bathroom shaving when he heard the phone ring. Thinking it was Lacey calling, he picked it up on the second ring. "Hello."

"Juan Carlos, is that you?"

He knew that voice and it wasn't Lacey's. "Yes, Sherlene! Why are you calling?"

"Well hello to you too!" Sherlene, his Acquisitions Attorney, was also like family to him and his brothers. Juan Carlos met Sherlene years ago, when he was at a seminar in New York City. She was the best in her field, was smart and ethical. Juan Carlos depended on her and she never failed him. Many would call her radical because in her spare time, she

157

championed the rights of those who would not or could not speak for themselves. She told it like it is, and was not afraid to stand up to Juan Carlos.

"Sherlene, please now is not a good time. Tell me what is it that you need?"

"Man, you are difficult to get in touch with. Greg called me hours ago. He warned me after saying you hung up on him! I've been calling your cell phone and left at least four messages. Are you ignoring me too?"

Juan Carlos was finding it difficult to concentrate on what Sherlene was saying. He needed to finish getting ready. Frustrated, yet practical, he said "it's not possible to ignore you!"

"Anyway, I'm calling about the negotiations for the acquisition. We are very close to sealing the deal. However, the CEO of Durante Olives wants your assurances you will not break up the company and fire the workers."

"We already made that promise! It's written into the terms and conditions you wrote, remember?"

"Juan Carlos, of course I remember. But he wants your assurances, in person!"

He sighed heavily. "I'm on an imposed vacation. Greg can handle it or the Board"

"Yes well, Durante asserts he will only sign off with you, and the Board unanimously agreed; they believe it shows our company is concerned for something other than money. You have to physically be there to shake on the deal."

"Oh okay! Now everyone wants me. It was fine to send me away. Until you needed me. I'll think it over and get back to you! Maybe tomorrow!"

"No, that won't work. The meeting is set for 6:00 PM today. That'll give you time to fly back this afternoon."

"What if I don't want to come back yet?"

It was Sherlene's turn to sigh. "Juan Carlos, you have to come back and make this deal happen. You're the only one who can. You cannot pout or let your anger get in the way. It is too important to the thousands of families depending on the company to keep them employed. You are the company!"

He conceded. "All right, you win! I'll be there!"

"Good, I'm glad you have come to your senses."

"Yeah, yeah, yeah." Have Greg make the arrangements and fax them to the hotel's business office. I'll pick them up within the hour."

"Will do! I'll see you this afternoon. And Juan Carlos? Don't forget to turn your cell phone back on!"

"Fine! Once the deal is signed, I'm coming back here to finish what I started."

" Uh huh, if you say so."

"Goodbye Sherlene!" He groaned as he slammed the phone down. What was he going to do? He did not want to leave Lacey at this fragile point in their relationship. Today he was going to convince her that they needed a more permanent relationship. He hadn't worked through his strategy just yet. Sherlene was right., He was the only one who could take this meeting. He just hoped Lacey would understand and still want to see him when he returned later tonight or tomorrow morning. He was running out of time and only had a few minutes to pack his business documents, laptop, and finish getting ready. In minutes, he'd gone from having lots of time to not having enough time.

Chapter 11

"A day without chocolate is a day without sunshine. Life without chocolate is like a beach without water." Source: *all about chocolate blogspot*

Lacey was on cloud nine when she sauntered into the hotel lobby. She was looking forward to another day with Juan Carlos. If he was willing to rearrange his life to spend more time with her, he must think her special. It had taken all her willpower not to whisper that she loved him yesterday. She almost caved and said it after he'd comforted her through her bad dream. But the last thing she wanted was to be labeled one of those 'clingy women' who misunderstood the nature of an affair. Just because he was nice to her in bed, did not mean they would have a relationship. She would take it one moment at a time and hope for the best.

When she saw Juan Carlos' face as he came into view, she knew something was wrong. He looked devastated. She hoped nothing was wrong with his family. He should not have ignored those phone calls. He had his overcoat and briefcase with him too. Coming across the lobby she stopped in front of him. "What's up? Something's happened!"

"Si, querida. I have to return to Barcelona now."

"Oh?" She questioned. She felt the tears fighting to make their presence known. No! She would not show weakness no matter how difficult this goodbye would be.

He rubbed his hand across his face. She could see he was frustrated. "We must postpone our day together. Unfortunately, I have to go back and close an important business deal."

"Okay, well it was nice to spend these days with you. Take care of yourself!" Lacey turned and started to walk away.

"Lacey, querida, wait!" He grabbed her arm to prevent her retreat. "Come, let's sit and talk for a few moments?" He pulled her over to the lobby lounge area and they sat down. He lifted her hand and kissed it. When he did that, she could not think; all logical thought went out the window.

"My Lacey, this is not how I wanted today to go. It cannot be helped. There is a company I am acquiring with thousands of people depending on me. I must take a meeting this evening to sign off and then I will return to Bruges. Back to you!"

"Juan Carlos, I understand. You do not have to explain or make me any promises. You are a busy man and business comes first. This was nice and I will treasure it always."

Her words cut him to his core. Business always comes first. Since he'd met her, he had rarely thought of business. She did not understand he needed her to see he was different. He lowered his head and kissed her. He did not know what words to choose. He immediately felt her resistance. She was building up her wall again. She was trying to shut him out. He did not stop kissing her until he felt her let him in. When he lifted his lips from hers, he said "Lacey, this is not goodbye for us. You matter too much to me. I will be back late tonight or tomorrow morning. Then we will pick up where we left off. Si querida?"

In a very quiet and controlled voice, she said "yes." She sounded unconvincing, even to herself.

In a quick move, he kissed her lips again and then rose from the couch. He looked down at her and she refused to meet his eyes. "I will be back as soon as humanly possible."

He watched Lacey twirl her fingers together on her lap and nod her head. Walking away from this woman, the woman he loved, was the hardest thing Juan Carlos had ever done. Damn business! What was life without someone to share it with. Lacey excited him in ways business and finance never would. He was forced to walk away to help those dependent on him. But there was no way he was going to stay away from the woman he loved!

******

When Lacey was sure he was gone, she ran from the lobby. By the time she had made it to the stairwell, hidden from view, the tears were coming down. She fell on the steps and cried. He would not be back. He was trying to let her down easy.

This day had been destined from the start. What she had with Juan Carlos was a weekend affair! Seeing him walk away hurt more than any other loss in her life. The love she had for her parents and Maria was 'family love' that a child has while they grow up. She had spent time with them; years in fact. With their death, while she was sad; the world expected her to go on and have a great life. Her love for Juan Carlos, even though it happened for her instantly when they met, it was about a man and a woman who connected on every level with passion and a heart-stopping love. Love had chosen her and

164

she was transformed. It hurt like hell that he left and she knew she would never again love anyone like she loved this man. What she needed was him. And if she could not have him, then she would have some chocolate. She pulled herself up from the steps and went in search of lots and lots of chocolate.

Chapter 12

Feeling like a rag doll, Lacey dragged herself up the steps in search of her room. When she walked through the door the only thing on her mind was how to ease the pain that seemed to have taken hold of her. Every breath was torture. A broken heart! She was in desperate need of chocolate. Looking about the suite and finding none, she discovered she had left the last of the box back in Juan Carlos' room.

This day was turning into a major nightmare. And it had begun like a fairy tale. She was the Princess and her sexy Prince Charming was catering to her every need and more. Why had she given in to the passion? Don't even go there...there is no room for regrets. Spending the afternoon and night in Juan Carlos' arms was a dream come true, and certainly more than any sane woman could possibly imagine would happen in reality!

Lacey began pacing back and forth. It was like she had renewed energy. Chocolate was the least of her problems. At least she would have no lack of options in replacing the box of chocolates. Juan Carlos, on the other hand, was irreplaceable. What to do with her pent-up energy? She did suppose that she needed a new chocolate stash, and then it was a new day in Bruges. The sun was up, and just because Lacey's lover had left did not mean she should take for granted that Bruges was still a magical city.

Time for a run. It would be refreshing and just maybe it would clear her head. There was no hope for easing her heartache this soon. One moment at a time Lacey would feel better. The day may come when she basked in the memories of how Juan Carlos changed her perception of this town. It had to be one of the most romantic places in the world. She had certainly fallen in love here. Too bad she would leave her heart here as well. Ah, but in the meantime, she had chocolate induced calories to burn and more chocolates to savor!

******

Juan Carlos arrived back in Barcelona just after two in the afternoon. He felt tension in his chest, and overwhelming guilt for walking out on Lacey. In the time it took him to get to Brussels, board a plane, and arrive home, he thought of little else. He had called the hotel three times and was unable to get in touch with her. He had not thought to ask for her cell phone number as she had been so accessible to him since the moment they met. He did not even know if she owned one and he forgot to leave his contact information. He could kick himself now for the oversight. Those were the details in life that all she had to do was smile at him and he would forget. He wanted to leave a message that said *I miss you*, but that seemed so impersonal. He had too much to say to her.

Stress lines formed on his forehead. Had she forgotten him that quickly? That was not possible. They had spent the most intensely enjoyable twenty-four hours together. Over the last few days, they had bonded in many ways. They talked so easily about everything. Sometimes he would lead and she would follow and vice versa. They had formed a partnership, even though they had yet to form words to define it. Before he returned to her, he needed to acquire an engagement ring. He would never leave her again without his ring on her finger or without her knowing how he felt. She was his, and they belonged with one another. So it would be.

Greg met Juan Carlos when he came off the jet way. He handed him a folder with the updated information on Durante Olives. "Juan Carlos, welcome home. Thank you for returning on such short notice. I know I was somewhat harsh with you at week's end, but..."

Juan Carlos held up his hand, "I understand. You were just following the Board's lead. Plus, I really do need time off."

Greg was speechless. He went to say something, but thought better of it. He did not know what was motivating Juan Carlos, but he much preferred this greeting over the wrath he feared would instead greet him this afternoon.

In the limousine, their discussions were all business. It was as if Juan Carlos had never been gone. Greg briefed him on the details of the meeting and dinner to follow. It would be a celebration to welcome Durante Olives into the Gutiérrez conglomerate. Just listening to Greg made him feel weary. It looked as if he would be unable to return to Bruges and Lacey tonight. He would try calling her again as soon as he got to his desk. Eventually she would return to her room and he would hear her voice.

Juan Carlos explained to Greg that he would be returning to Bruges early morning the next day. In the meantime, he needed to get to the office and catch up before the meeting.

"One more thing Greg. I need you to arrange a meeting with the jeweler for 5:00 PM this afternoon."

Greg often coordinated with the preferred jeweler to stop by the office when Juan Carlos needed to select a gift for family and friends. "What did you have in mind for selections?"

"Engagement rings."

"Juan Carlos, I do not think I heard you right. Did you say engagement rings?"

Juan Carlos looked up from his papers with amusement in his eyes. "Yes, that's correct. Something elegant, yet stylish."

Greg frowned. "Whom might the ring be for?"

"You sure are full of questions today Greg. The ring is for the woman I intend to marry."

Greg had picked up his glass of water and was sipping from it when Juan Carlos made his announcement. He literally choked on the contents. "What? Since when have you been interested in getting married. You're not even dating anyone. You are a workaholic. Remember it was you who said you had no time for relationships? Who are you planning to marry?"

"I met someone in Bruges. I did not mean to, but I fell in love."

"Have you gone mad? So, you met someone. Had a fling. That's great, but why are you irrationally talking about marriage. This is so not like you."

"I cannot imagine life without her. I have been gone from her for only hours and I am already feeling lost."

"Juan Carlos, you are a wealthy man. Are you sure she is not out for your fortune, status, or wanting you for some other less than savory reason? It is too soon for her to be pregnant, but you never know nowadays how far people are willing to go to get their way."

"Greg, you know me better than anyone else. Do you think I am an irrational man? Or that it is possible to take advantage of me? Lacey is not like that. I have thought this through. Once I set my mind on something, then I will figure out a way to have it. I know what I want, and I want her. If she will have me, then I will make her my wife."

"Wow! Congratulations, my friend. None of us could have thought this would happen as a result of a vacation. An affair, yes…a changed man, nada! However, I am nothing but excited that you have found something more important than business. I cannot wait to meet the woman who tamed you. I will arrange for the jeweler for 5:00 PM sharp."

The hours seemed to stretch on with pre-meeting activities, briefings, and paperwork. Juan Carlos had again tried to call the hotel numerous times. He was feeling desperation, almost panic-stricken and hoped nothing had happened to Lacey. Then he heard a knock on the door. Rubbing his hand over his face, he took a deep breath. "Come in."

His executive secretary, Martha, was at the door. "Sir, the jeweler has arrived. Should I send him in."

"Yes, please show him in."

Within fifteen minutes, Juan Carlos had found the perfect ring to brand Lacey to him. It was an emerald cut yellow diamond that reminded Juan Carlos of the fire that burned in her eyes. It was over three carats and set in a platinum setting. Surrounding the stone sparkled over one hundred small diamonds. He hoped she would like it and would think of him every time the light sparkled in the stones.

Once again alone in his office, he held the ring box in his hand. He picked up the phone and tried the hotel again. There was no answer so he decided to leave a voicemail message. He told her about his meeting and the dinner that would keep him from returning to Bruges until tomorrow. He apologized for spoiling their day but promised to make it up to her tomorrow. He left his phone numbers just so she could call him. He rang off suppressing the words I love you until he had the chance to say it the first time to her in person.

As soon as he hung up, his private line rang. Was it possible that she was calling back so quickly?

"Brother dear, we hear you are going to propose." It was Tomas Miguel's voice.

"Hola TM, who told you?" As one of the three brothers with two first names, Juan Carlos called his brothers Tomas Miguel and Leandro Cruz by their initials.

"It's true? No way!" His brother Javier spoke up.

"Oh, I see this is a community call. Hola Alberto, I suppose you are on the line too."

"Si, I was just trying to figure out who could possibly have weakened your resistance. One thing is for sure, better you than me."

Juan Carlos said, "for the first time in my life, I feel like there is so much more than business. I found a beautiful woman who is my soul mate."

Hearing Juan Carlos speak so seriously sobered his brothers that he had found 'the one.'

Javier piped in. "Congratulations bro! At least Mama will lighten up on us as soon as you take the plunge. We will have free reign while she pressures you for a grandchild." The three brothers agreed while laughing uncontrollably. "Wait till we tell the others!"

Juan Carlos was not amused. "Thanks, I think. Lacey and I will not be pressured into Mama's schedule."

That statement brought even more laughs. As the time approached 6:00 PM, Juan Carlos ended the call with his brothers. He was thankful Greg had called them as he wanted to share his news, but did not know how to start the conversation. With so many confirmed bachelors around him, it was an impossible subject. He was unlike them as he never focused on dating many women. He focused on making the company and family legacy successful. However, he knew Greg and his brothers were rarely without the company of some beautiful woman. It just never got serious.

As he rose from his desk on the way to the conference room, he wondered if he could convince Greg to tell his parents too. Mama would not be pleased that she did not get to approve of his fiancée before he proposed. He just hoped she would understand it was love at first sight and he could not wait to make her his wife. He would insulate Lacey with his love and that of a big family. After all, the most important thing was he had fallen in love and they would marry. One day when they decided the time was right they would have a child.

Chapter 13

"There is nothing better than a friend, unless it is a friend with chocolate." ~ Linda Grayson

The meeting with Mr. Durante concluded without incident. Dinner was a huge success and champagne flowed for many hours. Juan Carlos usually enjoyed these celebrations more than any other part of closing the deal. But tonight, he felt anxious to leave. The minutes seemed to drag on for too many hours. It was getting late and he wanted to try Lacey again. His flight would take off at 6:00 AM, and he would land in Bruges before breakfast ended. All he had to do was make it through the night and he would be holding Lacey for many nights to come.

******

Lacey was so tired of the phone ringing earlier in the day that she turned it off. She knew it had to be Juan Carlos intent on giving her the brush off over the phone versus doing it in person. She was not interested. Watching him walk away had been hard enough, that she was less than excited to hear him dump her. He was an admirable man who was true to his word. He would make some excuse as to why he would never see her again and then he would not feel guilty for telling her he would be back. If he wanted to do so, then he would have return tonight.

As the hours ticked up to midnight, she held out a bit of hope. The new box of chocolates sat untouched on the table. She did not have a taste for them. When the crying stopped, she reminisced on every word, kiss, and touch they'd shared. It made her breathless with longing. Now that the clock registered half past midnight, she realized it was not to be. *He's not coming back.* She turned over and shut off the bedside lamp. Sleep overtook her.

Lacey tossed and turned all night, and even awoke a couple of times to new nightmares. While the scenes were different, each was about losing Juan Carlos. The previous night while she slept in Juan Carlos' embrace, Lacey was convinced she was done with bad dreams. Reality said that she was not...

******

She sat in the window box of her room wrapped in her terry cloth robe and watched the sunrise just after 8:00 AM. She found it interesting she could see sunrise from her suite and sunset from Juan Carlos' bed. She wondered what he was doing this morning in Barcelona. If he was watching the same sunrise. When the beauty of the moment was done, she lifted the phone, ordered room service, then rose and headed for the bathroom to a hot shower. She heard her inner voice say *'would you snap out of this funk. I had enough of this yesterday. It is time to start a new day!'*

Just finishing drying her hair she heard a knock at the door. She was pleased she had timed her shower just perfectly, had finished her hair, and now her hot coffee was arriving. As she put her terry cloth robe on over her naked body, she even thought she might have a chocolate with her breakfast. Things were looking up!

She crossed the sitting room and opened the door. Instead of the room service cart and waiter, she saw Juan Carlos. He was standing there in a well-fitting, tailored Italian suit holding a bouquet of red roses and a box of chocolates. Lacey ran her tongue across he lips. *Damn he looks good.* "You're back…"

Juan Carlos took in the fact that she was again in that tempting terry cloth robe. He knew what lay beneath and his body stirred in excitement. "Querida, of course I'm back as I said I would be. Did you not get my message?" Juan Carlos looked over at the desk phone and saw the unobtrusive blinking light. Then he refocused on her. "Lacey, may I come in?"

"Please do." Lacey stepped aside and let him pass. She caught the faint smell of his unique scent and breathed in deeply. She never thought she would see him again.

He turned and handed her the roses and chocolates. "These are for you—the food and flowers of lovers." Lacey blushed, accepted the gifts and set them down on the table. As soon as her hands were free, Juan Carlos caught them and brought her to him. She was mesmerized by him being here. He placed her arms around his neck and he pulled her into his embrace. He leaned his head on her shoulder and whispered 'you are my delicate rose, Lacey. I missed you so much as I lived the longest hours of my life. While my flight landed in Brussels I watched the sun rise over the horizon. All I could wonder is whether you too saw the same sun.'

Tentatively she answered in a quiet voice, "I saw it. I missed you too. I thought you left me and were not coming back."

He lifted his head and looked into Lacey's eyes. "I thought you said you trusted me. I am always true to my word. I called many times, but you never answered. Finally, I had the sense to leave you a message." He looked back over to the desk phone. "I see you never listened to it. Why, querida?"

"I thought you were calling to tell me it was nice while it lasted, but you would not return."

Exasperated he said "you are such a hardheaded woman! Believe me, there was nothing that would stop me from returning to claim you." He looked from her eyes, to her lips. He lifted his thumb to rub it across her bottom lip. "To claim this." And then he put his lips on hers and passionately kissed her. She wrapped her arms tightly around his neck and melted into him.

When he withdrew from their kiss, she heard him curse under his breathe. 'Lacey, I could easily get carried away and take you to bed this moment. However, I need to tell you something."

His words shook her to the core. Was he going to end it now? She could not take much more of this emotional and physical heartbreak. It felt too good to be with him. To lose him again would be another crushing blow. Is this how real love felt? If they kept this up, she would surely be rendered insane before the month was out.

He captured her hand and brought her with him to the couch. Once he sat, he pulled her onto his lap. He rubbed his hand across his face. "Lacey, let me tell you a story. I came here to Bruges kicking and screaming. No, let me say that a different way. I was sent here to Bruges by my company who felt I needed to get away. Here in Bruges, I met a woman who changed my life. She took time out to guide me through town, and shared herself with me, including her prized chocolates. You see, I fell in love with a chocolate princess."

"What did you say?"

"Lacey, I know it is very soon in our meeting. But I love you. I did not plan for this to happen, but now I cannot imagine not being with you."

"But..."

"No Lacey, hear me out please. I wanted to tell you this yesterday, but I was called away too soon." He pushed an errant curl away from her face. "I hope you will stop struggling to suppress what could be in life. We have to live out our goals, hopes and dreams and refuse to succumb to our fears. We have to listen to our hearts when they speak."

She just nodded and he continued to speak. "Business has always been my life. I put it first, last, always. I was not opposed to loving someone, but did not execute a plan for it to happen. So, it was unexpected with you. You make me love chocolate. It is one of your passions for life. I wanted that passion for something or someone other than work. I have it now because of you. Will you marry me Lacey?"

In a fog, Lacey answered in a squeaky voice, "What?"

Not quite the response he'd hoped for. "We are friends and have connected on so many levels. Maybe I will not attain an equal par with chocolate, but I still want to be in your life. Don't give up on love and what is possible. Don't give up on me. I have enough love for both of us. I want you to be my wife. Will you marry me?" Out of nowhere came a black box he'd opened. It held the most exquisite ring she had ever seen. It was a yellow diamond encased by lots of smaller diamonds.

Taking a deep breath and inching a little bit closer to him, Lacey said, "yes, I will marry you."

It was Juan Carlos' turn to question. "Si? Yes? Are you sure, querida?"

"Yes, I'm sure. I love you so much, and I have since you walked into that chocolate shop. Now will you shut up and kiss me." And he did. He gently pushed her back on the sofa and in a moment of desperate need to kiss her, he placed his lips against hers. She opened her mouth to him and he branded her. He said, "you belong to me forever." When they came up to breathe, he put his ring on her finger and whispered into her ear, "I want to see you in my ring and nothing else."

It took Juan Carlos the rest of that reunion day to convince Lacey that they should get married the upcoming weekend so they could start their honeymoon as soon as possible. He'd already researched that it was next to impossible to get married in Bruges without six months' notice. He confessed he had five more weeks' time off so they had the means and resources to go anywhere. So, he asked her what was her next favorite place she would love to show him. She told him the Caribbean island of Antigua. The sun and people had such warmth that said *welcome home.* Also, it has 365 beaches, one for every day of the year! The idea brought a smile to his face. He was anxious to visit as many of those beaches as possible and just might make memories with his bride on each one...

Epilogue

"Your love is better than chocolate."
~ *Author: Sarah McLachlan*

Early the following Saturday morning half the world away from Bruges, they eloped in a civil ceremony on the small island of Antigua, just the two of them. He had only told Greg his plans. Juan Carlos knew there would be hell to pay from Mama, but this was the best way to claim Lacey as his forever. He planned to have a religious blessing in his family's church and big reception when they returned to Spain in the weeks to come.

Lacey was beautiful on this, their special day. She wore a white wrap dress he insisted she had to wear for him when she'd modeled her new warm weather purchases. It reminded him of her in a terry cloth robe. That was a sight he could never get enough of, nor the feeling of unwrapping it from her body. As soon as they returned to their home, she would find he'd purchased many similar wrap dresses in an array of colors. Hell, she never needed to get dressed as far as he was concerned. She also wore an amber tear drop necklace and matching earrings he'd given her last night. *Oh, last night was*

184

memorable watching sunset on Jolly Beach! Just 364 left to visit...

His attention was brought back to present with her sweet voice. In the center of their bridal villa with champagne glasses at hand, his Lacey said to him: "In the end, I will forever love chocolate, but I will no longer rely on it. More valuable than anything to me, I have you, my Juan Carlos, mi amour. With you I am no longer afraid. The love that has grown between us will live forever and not even death can ever diminish it." She smiled as she popped a white chocolate truffle into her mouth, and he kissed her lips...

The End

About the Author:

L. Elaine lives in Maryland, just outside her hometown of Washington, DC. She has three sons, a daughter-in-law-to-be, and a granddaughter, whose eyes sparkle each time she gets a new idea!

Almost a decade ago, with coaxing from a dear friend at work, she decided to write her own romance novel to see if she would enjoy crafting beautiful stories of love set in exotic locales. And she does, so she continues to write!

Besides reading and writing, L. Elaine enjoys traveling, teaching, meeting people and tasting food from foreign lands. She considers herself a lifelong learner with lots left to discover! She would love to hear from you so please visit her website.

EXCERPT

from the next book
in the series
Dynasty of Love

The Gutiérrez Family: Book 2

And stay tuned for more love stories from the
Dynasty of Love series about the Gutiérrez
family!

Javier and Olivia's Story...excerpt:

Javier searched the beach just over the rise from his beach house as he steered his helicopter. Olivia said she would be spending the morning soaking up the sun rays at the water's edge. Not quite sure why she would pick the beach over the pool, he smiled as he thought of how they had made love in the pool lounger yesterday afternoon. Reigning in those thoughts, he looked at his watch to verify the time. Yes, as the big hand moved just to 11 o'clock, he was sure it was still   morning.

"Where is she?" He said speaking out loud as he knew she would not go back on her word. He picked up his binoculars to get a better view.

Scanning the sandy dunes, he saw her in the distance. No one else would be around on the private beach. There she lay sprawled across the beach chair in a flimsy white dress with her hair flowing free. One look at her instantly excited him. She looked to be reading some sort of book or magazine from behind dark sunglasses. The material of her dress was so gauzy and lightweight that he could clearly make out her shape beneath it. Knowing her wild streak, he was sure the temptress had little or nothing on under it.

188

At that moment, all he wanted to do was land the helicopter right there next to her in the sand and make passionate love to her for the rest of the day. Olivia was a vixen who haunted his thoughts and dreams. He could not get enough of her. This tryst was in no way close to being practical and yet felt alive in her presence for the first time in years, maybe the first time ever. She gave as good as she took, and he was having all kinds of adventures with her inside and outside of his private beach house. Today would be no different...

39670409R00115

Made in the USA
Middletown, DE
22 January 2017